Born to Dance
SAMBA

Born to Dance

SAMBA

by Miriam Cohen

Drawings by Gioia Fiammenghi

1 8 17

———————— HARPER & ROW, PUBLISHERS ————————

Cambridge, Philadelphia, San Francisco, London, Mexico City, São Paulo, Sydney

———————————— NEW YORK ————————————

BORN TO DANCE SAMBA
Text copyright © 1984 by Miriam Cohen
Illustrations copyright © 1984 by Gioia Fiammenghi
All rights reserved. No part of this book may be used or reproduced in any manner whatsoever
without written permission except in the case of brief quotations embodied in critical articles
and reviews. Printed in the United States of America. For information address Harper & Row,
Publishers, Inc., 10 East 53rd Street, New York, N.Y. 10022. Published simultaneously in Canada
by Fitzhenry & Whiteside Limited, Toronto.
Designed by Joyce Hopkins
1 2 3 4 5 6 7 8 9 10
FIRST EDITION

Library of Congress Cataloging in Publication Data
Cohen, Miriam.
Born to dance samba.

Summary: At Carnival time in Brazil, a girl who has
spent her life wishing to be chosen Queen must cope
with the jealousy incurred by a new girl who is her only
competition.
[1. Carnival—Fiction.   2. Brazil—Fiction]
I. Fiammenghi, Gioia, ill.   II. Title.
PZ7.C6628Bo 1984   [Fic]   83-47690
ISBN 0-06-021358-2
ISBN 0-06-021359-0 (lib. bdg.)

For all my wonderful teachers:
Maria Muniz (in Brazil), Katherine Paterson,
Charlotte Zolotow, Jan Aldrich, Susan Hirschman,
Elizabeth Shub, George Williams, Gay Courter,
and Monroe Cohen

Born to Dance

SAMBA

1

"Teresinha, you think you're so much with all that hair. It's probably got fleas in it." I put in some fat ones, like raisins. "And why do you have such a pinchy, stingy little nose?" I drew that in too. "The way you dance, you just jump around looking stupid. What did you want to come to our Hill for? Huh?!... You've got nothing to say? Okay. You asked for it!" I crumpled Teresinha up and threw her off the cliff. "And you better not try hanging around here with my gang!"

Teresinha's picture bounced over the rocks and stubby bushes, out into the blue air and down, down, down. It

was falling into the green-and-purple ocean, but I couldn't see it hit. Our Hill is too high in the sky for that.

"Hey, Maria Antonia!" Nilton came up the path pulling his wagon behind him. It was made out of a crashed baby buggy and wheels from three different bicycles, with a Brazilian flag stuck in front. When he'd parked it in his uncle's yard, he came the rest of the way up.

I flopped on my back and sighed, "Aiiii," like "The Most Miserable Lady in Rio Today" on T.V. ("The Most Miserable Lady" is the one they pick to be on T.V. because her husband left her, her kids are all in jail (except the baby), and she has just been run over by an express bus.) "Two weeks! How can I wait so long? I can't. I won't wait for Carnival anymore!"

"You'll wait. Everybody waits." Nilton lay down with his hands behind his head. I chewed on a piece of grass. . . .

"My Gramma already waited fifty-eight times because she's fifty-eight years old. Every year when Carnival's over, she says, 'Hurry up! Hurry up! Only eleven more months to get ready for the Procession.' "

"Your Gramma's like a little kid." Nilton said.

"Yeah, she's like a little kid." I smiled, thinking of Gramma. The hem on my dress was coming down. I pulled out some more stitches.

"Nilton, do you think Teresinha is a very good dancer?"

"Yes."

"As good as me?"

5

"Maybe yes, maybe no."

"Well, in the Procession, do you think Teresinha will get picked for Star of the Kids?"

"She could be."

"She won't be! I know she won't!"

"Why ask me if you know? And how could you know that anyway?"

"I know."

"How can you tell what the Director will decide?"

"I know but I can't tell you."

Nilton lifted his eyebrows and lay back again. Flopping on my stomach, I told myself, *Don't worry, honey. It's sure to be you.*

Nilton lay with his eyes closed as though he were sleeping. But if someone was throwing away an old icebox on the other side of the Hill, Nilton would know it. I poked him. "Nilton, are you born lucky?"

"Who? Me?"

"No—anybody."

"Some people are born lucky."

"But can you lose the luck after you're born with it?"

Nilton looked at me. "If you're lucky, you don't lose it."

That's what I thought too. It made me feel good again. Closing my eyes, I just let the sky slide over me and The Hill of the Cashew Tree hold me up for a while.

I wasn't looking, but I could see Rio, as if I were flying over it. I zoomed around the giant blue hills pushing themselves out of the ocean. I swam in the air between the tall, white apartments. And I dived down close to the little, wooden put-together houses holding on so they wouldn't fall off the hills.

Lots of kids were playing around those little houses. With my magic eyes, I could see inside their heads. If they're boys, they think they're going to be great soccer stars like Pelé. If they're girls, they dream they're going to be the Queen of the Samba. Flying away, back to my Hill, I called from the sky, "Girls, don't think I'm stuck-up! But your dream is already taken—by *me*, Maria Antonia Carmen dos Santos!"

You see, I was born dancing, and I was born lucky. I was born to be Queen of the Samba! Nobody can take it away from me, not even that Teresinha.

"Wouldn't it be good, Nilton, if you could just wish a person wouldn't be there anymore? You just look hard at them and, *Blam!* they're gone. I don't mean hurting her, that is, this person . . . Nilton?" He was gone. Maybe there *was* an icebox on the other side of the Hill, and Nilton was there unscrewing the door handle to sell. That's how he gets the small change he always has in his pocket.

It's all right. I don't mind. I'm used to it. When I'm alone, I just start the movie. It's always there, behind my eyes—"The Night on the Avenue." Everybody from our Hill is in it, laughing and singing, dancing like pink-and-green fire. Pearls and diamonds are blinking all over

7

the Kings and Queens, the assistant Kings and Queens, the Lords and Ladies, the shepherdesses, and the acrobats. People are shiny with sweat and smiling like they can never stop. And there I am, in front of them all! I'm wearing the cutest costume! It's the color of a raspberry Popsicle with green sparkles on it. And I'm dancing like . . . I *am* . . . the Queen of the Samba! (I'm still this eleven-year-old size though.)

I never tell anyone about it; you have to be careful. Nilton said you can't lose your luck, but it's better not to boast about it. You might make it go away, even though you're very sure. And I'm sure, because there are certain signs that tell it's going to be me.

I can remember *before* I was born. Yes, when Mama danced Samba, inside I was dancing too. There was a teeny hammock in there, and I could lie down when I got tired because, of course, I was very little. It's true! I even remember where we were, though I couldn't see out. It was on the white pavement with lights all around, where we rehearse for Carnival. (I never told anybody except Gramma about this, and she believes me.)

Well, because of that time inside, I've had more practice than any other kid. I'm going to be Queen—I feel it in my soul. And that's the most important place, right here, between your heart and your stomach.

Besides, my sisters and brothers each have their own special luck. Regina is the prettiest, like a T.V. star. She's

8

always smiling because it's lucky to be so pretty. "Come over here, little sister," she says. "I'll fix your hair so it's longer." And she lends me her earrings so I can sit on the steps, shaking my head to jingle them. Alberto and Roberto, my two big brothers, are smart and handsome. They can get any jobs they want. And Maria Helena is such a good reader that she's going to be a schoolteacher, while Maria Clara is going to get married. That's all she wants, to be a wife, even though she's the best dancer on our Hill. Carlos comes just before me and he's a rat. But he's a champ with the soccer ball. Oh! The baby, Little Sergio—what his luck is he's too small to tell.

Now me, my face isn't much and my hair is just a little frizzle in a ponytail, but I can dance, I can *really* dance. At rehearsals, the grown-ups stop to watch. "Look at that little girl of Tomas and Elisabete's. She was born to dance! She's going to grow up to lead the Procession, just you wait." This belongs to *me*. It's *my* luck. I'm going to be the Queen. That's the best in the whole world you can be. You aren't some funny-looking little kid anymore. You are beautiful because you dance so beautiful. Everyone knows about you, and you are the leader of the people.

So, how can I help it? I dream that it's me carrying the flag, turning and dipping, smiling while the people shout, "Bravo, Maria Antonia! Bravo, The Cashew Tree!"

Oh, don't you worry—it's going to be me. Before I was born, it was already decided.

"Maria Antonia! Where is my bleach?!" Mama sounded mad. She sent me to buy a bottle of bleach a long time ago.

"I'm going! Right now, I'm going!" It made more holes in them, but I sat on my panties and slid down the Hill.

Nilton is my boyfriend. You don't believe I have a boyfriend? Well, neither did I, because as I told you my face
is not a bit pretty. But since we were really little, we just
took hands and went around together.

It's not that kissing kind of business of course! It's
just that I always look for him if he isn't there, and he
is always coming around here to see me. My friend Louisa
says, "He's terribly good-looking!" But he never goes
with any other girl. So, he *is* my boyfriend, and I think
it will always be like that.

This morning he said, "Maria Antonia, let's go to the beach."

"Just us?"

"Yes, come on. I want to test my underwater goggles."

Nilton had some old sunglasses without the glass. He put the bottoms from plastic soda bottles in the frames with chewed chewing gum to hold them against his face and keep out the water. Nilton's very good at thinking of these things.

"I couldn't go without a grown-up. Mama thinks I'll drown. She'd never let me go."

"Ask her to come. Tell her to bring the baby. We'll hold his hands, and he can put his toes in the water."

"She'll never do it. She'll say she has too much work. And she'll send me to the store."

"Ask her."

We went inside. Mama's face was sweating, and her hair was coming down in straggles from her bobby pins. This morning I washed all the baby's diapers for her. Gramma usually did that, but our neighbor Carolina had swollen legs, and Gramma was helping her. So I prayed Mama would say "Yes."

"Please, can we all go to the beach? We'll pull the baby in Nilton's wagon, and we'll take care of him, and you won't have to do a thing."

She pushed back her hair. "I have too much work to do." I poked Nilton. Then her eyes seemed to see the cold, shiny water. And she said, "Well, if we came back quickly, before it's time for Poppa to come home . . ."

Before she could change her mind, we put a towel in a shopping bag, a fan, and Pop's straw hat to shade Mama's face. "Hurry, hurry, Mama, please," I begged. "So we won't have to come back right away!"

Down the Hill we started. Mama carried the baby because she didn't trust Nilton's wagon. He left it by his uncle's place. Halfway to the bottom, she was worrying that she shouldn't have gone away from her house. But we helped her up the steps of the bus before she could change her mind.

We got off when we got to the City so Mama could look in the shop windows. Nilton and I slipped around the gray suits of the businessmen and flew by the heavy ladies carrying their heavy shopping bags. We were at the end of a block before Mama had even started. We couldn't wait!

Past the high buildings, the different, lighter air was telling us, "Here! The beach is here. And the ocean is waiting!"

Again and again we ran back, circling around Mama, trying to help her walk faster. We were so afraid she'd say, "I never should have come."

Our family goes to the beach only a few times every year. It's far. And think how much bus fare it would take for all of us! Besides, Poppa is always working, and the brothers and sisters too. Some kids, like Nilton, go by themselves anytime. I would try it, but you couldn't hide

13

where you'd been from Mama. You'd be too clean.

"Nilton! Where is she? I don't see Mama and Little Sergio!" The people in the streets filled up so quickly the place where my mother had been. Back we ran till we saw the soft, old pink of Mama's dress and Little Sergio's round, black eyes peeping over her shoulder. She was looking in a store window.

It was a souvenir store where tourists buy things to take home. Not pots and pans, or rubber sandals, or T.V.s, but things you couldn't use: a skin of an animal with spots, Indian spears, glass pictures with huge, shiny blue butterflies inside. "Are they real?" Nilton said they were, but I never saw such butterflies. Only somebody's gown at Carnival could be so blue, somebody with a big part.

"What is it? What are you looking at, Mama?" She showed us little brown people pinched out of clay and dried. A dentist pulled the tooth of a yelling man. A lady and her boyfriend danced, holding each other far apart. A teacher was teaching some grown-ups how to spell, and they were scratching their heads. A family walked somewhere in a line with pots and pans and bundles on their heads. Even their parrot was riding on top.

"Why are you looking at these funny little country people, Mama?"

She shook her head and turned away. "I'm finished."

Finally we crossed the last avenue and ran out onto the black-and-white, curvy sidewalk by the beach. They

14

put the black-and-white bits of stone in the sidewalk to look just like the waves in the ocean. Nilton and I held our arms out. We were going to hug the ocean! "The ocean! The ocean!" we shouted.

The ocean was playing with the beach. It shook its head and roared and jumped on the sand, then slid back with a pebbly laugh. "Were you scared? I was just playing!"

A thousand people, brown like cinnamon, walked on the white sand. Their bathing suits painted red, purple, green, and orange on the white.

I held the baby for Mama, and she took off her shoes to walk more easily in the sand. "Let's go there, by the rocks, where the water is quiet." Nilton pointed.

"Don't those rocks look like big fish pulled out of the water?" I asked. "Doesn't the water look like green Jell-O?"

"Everything doesn't look like something else. It looks like itself," Nilton said.

"Anyway, Mama, here's a nice place. Put your things down and sit on the towel with Little Sergio. Here's your hat so the sun doesn't give you a headache. Nilton and me will be right back."

You can swim just as good in your regular clothes. Then you don't have to bother about changing into bathing suits. Sometimes I wish I had a purple elastic one that ties around your neck, with a ruffle on the panties. But my Carnival costume is pretty enough.

15

Kicking our feet high, we ran and threw ourselves into the ocean. Nilton kept on going. He ducked under and only the bottoms of his feet showed where he was. I stayed where the littler waves catch you and make you scream, you like it so much.

I could see Mama, sitting up straight with her legs in front of her and her skirt pulled tight over her knees. Little Sergio patted the sand. "Mama! Watch this!" Pinching my nose I sat all the way under, to the bottom. Then I jumped up and splashed toward the beach. "Mama, I'm coming to play with Little Sergio."

Nilton was coming out of the water too. "Did the goggles work? What did you see with them?"

"I have to think of something else. The chewing gum didn't stay, and the water came in."

We flopped down next to Mama and began to build a tunnel for the baby. He laughed when Nilton's foot wiggled through it.

"Mama, why don't you lie down and rest?"

There were oiled, bare ladies lying all around. They kept their eyes closed, and their red fingernails brushed away any sand from their soft, brown stomachs.

She wouldn't, we knew she wouldn't, but Nilton and I wiggled ourselves into the hot sand. "Mama, did you come to the beach when you were a kid?"

"No, no. In the Northeast there was no beach. There was no water. In the backlands, where we lived, it was dry. So dry the people had to move all the time, looking

16

for water. We had to leave our house, with the little fig tree—we couldn't take it of course—and go on the road, trying to find some food and water. It was very bad. We came in a truck to the City, to Rio, and it was better then.

"I got married to your Poppa. And I remember he took me to the movies for the first time in my life. I couldn't believe such a beautiful place as that theater! I didn't want to go out when the picture was over. And all the fruits and meats and vegetables! You could walk right up and buy them! Sometimes I'm afraid about moving again, with everything on our heads, like the little dry people in the store window. . . ."

Nilton and I looked at each other. My mother never told these things before. "Well," I said, "it can't happen again because this is Rio. And you have Pop and all your sons and daughters to work for you. And some of us might be famous T.V. stars or Queen of the Samba, and we'd always take care of you and Poppa."

Mama smiled and began gathering up the towel and our sleeping baby. "It's late. If the beans are burned, I don't know what I'll do! Gramma forgets a lot, you know." She frowned. "What got into me today?!" Nilton carried the baby, and we went slowly toward the sidewalk.

The tall apartments took the rich people back up into them. The hot-gold sun cooled itself in the ocean. Over the sand hurried the Kibon Man. His customers were leaving with the sun. Nilton and I couldn't help looking

18

after him, even though we didn't want Mama to think she should buy us a sweet, cold red Popsicle, or a little vanilla cup.

"Run after him! Get three cups!" Mama was unpinching her little plastic purse and counting out the money. "Kibon Man! Wait! Wait!" I held out my arms for the baby, and Nilton ran after him.

"Here." Nilton gave Mama one cup, me another, and the baby the last one.

"No, no." Mama put hers into his hand. "The baby and I will eat this one. It's much too much for Little Sergio. And I hardly like ice cream at all."

Nilton and I took little wooden spoonfuls so it would last. Mama spooned big ones into Little Sergio, so vanilla was all around his mouth and on his nose. In between Mama licked the spoon. We scratched and scraped on the bottom of the cups till there wasn't a bit more.

Then we crossed between the cars on the avenue and started back to our Hill.

The morning after we went to the beach, Mama worked and worked. (I think she was "spanking" herself for going.) We cleaned and shook out the beds till I was glad to be sent to Lindomar's store. Outside, I watched the people, always going up or coming down this Hill.

Isabella's head, with a tin of water on top, was coming up the path. Then her round, nice fronts and then her strong, bare feet. She kept so steady that not a drop splashed out of the tin. (I must carry a bigger tin with more water so my legs will get stronger for dancing.)

Maria came down with her twins. Their fat little behinds rode on each side of her. Rubber nipples stuck in their mouths till Adolfo dropped his. What a hollering came out! Then Augusto cried and dropped his too. I was going to help, when Dona Elena came, hurrying out of her big, old sneakers. "Cootchie, cootchie," she said to the twins and put their stoppers back in. If a baby is crying a mile away, Dona Elena comes. She's very weird, but she's crazy about babies.

Mama was waiting. I jumped off the step and ran, past Auntie Serafina on her little porch, rocking and smiling and greeting everybody. "Hi, darlin'!" She waved. "Hi, Auntie!" I yelled over my shoulder.

Uncle Herman's underpants were jumping and kicking on the clothesline. Maybe they could still feel Uncle Herman dancing Samba in them. Now I was running and leaping like a crazy bird; the Hill makes you go faster and faster toward the bottom. And *Poom!* a big rubber pillow came up the path and smacked into me!

"Ufff! No respect! No respect!" The rubber pillow talked! I looked up—at Mr. Alberto Nascimento, and he was MAD!

"Who do you think you are, racing around here like a wild boy?! These pesty kids!"

Who do I think I am?! *Not* one of those pesty kids! I'm different! You'll see someday! I didn't say this out loud, of course, but ducking past, I stuck out my tongue at his back. He's so full of himself! And his nickname, "Rubber Stomach"—it's true!

21

Somebody was laughing.

"Nilton, you shut up!" It was him, I knew it, behind his uncle's house. Nilton always laughs. When the police come looking for someone, Nilton climbs higher like a monkey and throws jokes down on them. It's dangerous, but that's how he is. "Stop laughing, Nilton!" I ordered.

"I'm not laughing at you." Nilton came out from behind his uncle's house.

Poking out his stomach, Nilton walked along smiling as if he were in love with himself—just like Mr. Nascimento! Then he ran around, and he was *me*, butting into Mr. Nascimento with my head! It was very funny how Nilton could do that, but I wasn't going to laugh.

"You pineapple head! Come down with me to Lindomar's. I have to buy squashes for my mother."

At the bottom of the Hill, Nilton began laughing again. "Why are you laughing now? You always think something is funny—it's so stupid!"

"Maybe I was thinking of Mr. Nascimento—maybe I just like to laugh."

Bossy and mean, that's what I was being. Mama says, "That child can be bossy and mean!" Once I laughed all the time too. But now there is this worry, like gas in the stomach. I think the worry about Teresinha is making me this way.

"Have you got something for me?" Arnaldo was waiting by Lindomar's store. He's twenty-six years old, but

22

he's like a kid. He always wants a present. It didn't have to be much, so I felt in my pocket and took out a button with real gold on it. For a second I held it—"Oh, here, you can have it." Arnaldo smiled a big smile and went away holding the button tight. Nilton didn't, but some kids would say, "What a stupid that Arnaldo is!"

Lindomar's wooden store is very small. And Lindomar is a *big*, fat lady with a mustache. She sits inside on a stool and leans out to wait on her customers. Without getting up, she just reaches over her head or to the side for a box of matches, a package of dark-smelling coffee, or a scoop from a pointed mountain of soft, white flour. Close around her is anything you could ever need— empty gasoline tins to carry water, crooked green squashes with little hairs on them, and all kinds of soaps and scrubbers for dishes and laundry.

"If she ever gets up, the store will have an earthquake," Nilton whispered.

I thought of Lindomar at Carnival. Her costume has an enormous satin skirt that can go all the way around her and still puff out at the sides. And she carries this great big basket of fruits on her head. She rocks along so easy! It's like the ferry in the harbor was dancing Samba. "She's big as a ferryboat, but she can really dance," I whispered back.

Jercino, the garbage man, was buying squashes too. Once I saw him down in the City, with the men from his truck, sitting on the curb, beating out Samba on the bottoms of their garbage cans. Now he was squeezing and pinching the squashes, looking for the best ones. When she saw him, Lindomar shouted, "Pinch me! Don't pinch my squashes!" Who would dare pinch Lindomar?

"Where is your husband, Mrs. Lindomar?" Jercino asked. "I want to dicuss with him that part in the story where Alfonso Sambas into the center." Lindomar moved herself on the tiny stool. (The stool was there, we knew, though we couldn't see it.)

"He was just here."

Nilton whispered, "She might be sitting on him, poor little man." I started to giggle, then I remembered Lindomar chasing kids like a giant bear, waving her paws and cussing.

She noticed us waiting and chuckled in her throat; it sounded like the oil pouring out of the big barrel in her store. "Kids! Are you practicing so you can be the Flag Bearer and her Escort when you grow up?" Nilton grinned and shrugged. I looked hard at Lindomar, then I looked down. Did it show?! Could Lindomar tell somehow that standing right in front of her was the next Queen of the Samba?!

Jercino finished squeezing and said, "Fifty cruzeiros! And that's my last offer!"

"Fifty-five, and these beautiful squashes are yours." She was already wrapping them.

"Mrs. Lindomar, my mother wants two pounds of squash," I said.

Hugging the squashes, I hurried with Nilton up the path. Now I *might* have to take care of Teresinha. I didn't want to, but I *might* have to beat her up. She shouldn't be allowed to make the Queen of the Samba nervous!

"You look weird," Nilton said. "What are you thinking?"

"Nothing. We better go fast because my Mama's going to be mad."

Nilton and I jumped up the Hill "like a pair of goats." (That's what we look like, Pop says.) We rushed into the house, and I dumped the squashes on the table with a lot of noise so Mama could see I was hurrying. She turned from ironing Pop's costume. "What am I going to do with this child?! If she could Samba to the store, I'd have no trouble getting squashes."

Gramma was smiling with all her wrinkles at Nilton and me. Nilton was right; Gramma is like a little kid. When she laughs, she shows one tooth in her pink gums, like the baby, Little Sergio. Maybe she got so old she started to get young again? It would be so good if Gramma really was getting young again—then she would never die! But I don't *ever* think about that. I took the baby from the bed and hugged and kissed him. "Does this little Mousie want to get tickled?" My fingers danced over his stomach, and Nilton kept falling down so the baby would laugh.

After a while, we put Sergio—holding tight to his bottle—on the bed. Then we lay back and gazed at the walls. Nilton and I like to do that. My sisters pasted them all over with magazine pictures: lots of fat children from the City with short pink dresses so their panties would show, and tight, little blue shorts. There were older girls on the beach too, smiling and taking a deep breath so their chests would stick out.

"Don't those little kids get tired of looking so cute?" I asked Nilton.

His finger touched a shiny blue car. It had no roof so the happy people in it could wave to the people who didn't have cars. "I wouldn't get tired of *that*," Nilton said.

"This girl is much prettier than Teresinha." I pointed to one with a teeny red bathing suit. "I bet she can dance better too." Nilton kept looking at the car. It makes me mad! He just won't say anything bad about Teresinha.

Outside the window it was getting darker. "Maybe Pop is coming right now. Let's go watch for him!" We jumped up and ran out the door, leaping over all the steps to the ground.

"Come home as soon as Poppa comes! Supper is ready!" Mama called after me.

"Yes, yes! I know, I know!"

When we came to where the path falls over and down, we dropped on our stomachs and looked to see if Pop was coming up. Nilton's Pop went away a long time ago, maybe to Bahia. It was no use looking for him.

"Hey, wait! I'll show you the singing birds I caught in the woods." Nilton did three flips frontward and three backward ones to his uncle's house—the one made of all-colored boards. His uncle found them in the City, because they are crashing down the houses there to make more apartments. Nilton stopped to talk to Aristotle, his uncle's black-and-white spotted goat. "How's life, old hairy man?" Then he did another flip into the open door. "Bak! Bak! Bak!" His aunt's chickens came running out, cussing at Nilton.

Putting my chin on my hands, I gazed all around. Our Hill is so high, higher than the President's Palace. Far, far over there, the sky was getting lost in the dark, and the other hills were coming closer. No—they weren't hills! They were giant Kings and Queens, walking to Carnival over the purple water. For costumes, they wore black velvet capes. And the lights of the cars were the jewels going around the hems.

"Here." Nilton came back, holding the small wood

28

cage he had carved. I could hardly see the birds, it was getting so dark, but I knew they were plain little ones, gray and brown. "They won't sing now. You can hear them before I sell them tomorrow." I wished Nilton didn't put birds in a cage to sell. But it's a way to get money.

"Hey, Nilton!" Sebastian and Louisa and Hambone and John from the Northeast jumped out of the dark. "Make them sing, Nilton!"

"Nobody can make birds sing. Anyhow, birds don't sing when it's night."

Sebastian cussed, not that he wanted to hear the birds so much; he just liked to cuss. The kids threw themselves on the ground. Right away Louisa began to fix my ponytail, snapping the rubber band on and off.

"I saw Teresinha today, Maria Antonia. She was walking around, showing off her hair again."

"You're always saying things about her, and you don't even know her," Nilton said.

"Huh! Who'd want to? She's so stuck-up!" we both told him. Louisa went back to playing with my hair.

"Is your costume ready? Teresinha's is and it's so cute!"

"Gramma promised it will be ready for the Friday rehearsal," I said.

The only one they could choose for Star of the Kids is me, or that Teresinha. She doesn't belong on our Hill, but everybody says, "That Teresinha is pretty. That Teresinha can dance like a little devil." Her hair is the good kind, long and wavy. Not like mine—I touched my pony-

29

tail—just a little bunch of crinkly hairs. I've grown it and grown it, and Mama combs it hard and puts on Sof 'n' Long hair cream, but it's still the same, short and full of little bumps.

Hambone was bragging, "I never go to bed the whole four days and nights of Carnival."

"Baloney!" shouted John from the Northeast. "Last year I saw you sleeping on the sidewalk downtown!"

"Who cares about that?" Louisa asked. "What's important is, who's going to be Star of the Kids? I wish it would be me, dancing in front of the judge and everybody yelling 'Hey, Louisa!' But it's not gonna be me, I know it." Nobody said anything because that was true. Louisa wasn't good enough to be the Star.

"It's going to be me." The words just jumped out of my mouth before I could stop them!

"How do you know?" Hambone asked.

"It's supposed to be me. There are certain reasons."

"It could be Teresinha," the kids said, and they looked at one another.

"The Director is the only one that knows. Probably it's you, but it *might* be Teresinha," Nilton said.

"You'll see," I said. "There are certain things that prove it will be me."

"What things?" the kids wanted to know.

I kept saying, "You'll see. You'll see."

You mustn't boast about your luck. I couldn't tell them anything more. But there was my movie—me, alone in the front; people saying, "Who *is* that little dancer? My, how she can Samba!"

"Certain things? What things? You're crazy!" Sebastian laughed.

John from the Northeast said, "Teresinha's fast, and besides, *she's* good-looking."

That made me so mad! I screamed, "Go stick beans up your nose! You're talking to the Queen!" Everybody became silent.

"Hey, Maria Antonia!" Pop had come up the Hill without us seeing. He stood smiling at me.

"I'm tired of talking to you dummies!" I told them and jumped up. What a good time for Pop to come! Pop bent down for a kiss. He didn't have to bend far; he's a little Pop, but a strong one.

I took his arm. "Are you tired, Pop?" Pop drives an enormous rushing bus in the City, and it's very hard work.

"All I need is a little Samba at rehearsal tonight and 'Magic!' I'm not tired anymore." Pop grinned down at me.

"Give me that, Pop." With one hand I reached for his bundle, and with the other I held his hand carefully so as not to make him more tired.

We walked slowly along. *Don't worry, honey. It doesn't matter if Teresinha is prettier. You're the only one. The born dancer is you!* It was like somebody inside me said that! Pop was nodding "good evening" to the other people

31

coming home until we reached the little white fence he had put around our house.

I'll say I never said that about being Queen. Those dumb kids made me do it!

Pop bent to straighten one of the sticks. He is very proud of his fence. We don't have any yard; the little white sticks go right against the house, but it looks nice. Of course, the fence isn't to keep anybody from coming. People run in and out all day, and the houses lean close like they're talking too. So, everybody knows everything about everybody else on The Hill of the Cashew Tree.

Through the window we could see all the things happening in our house. Mama stirred the bean stew, but she wasn't seeing it. Her eyes were looking far away. My little brown Gramma was almost buried in pink-and-green satin. She was sewing still another ruffle on Maria Clara's costume. Alberto, my biggest brother, was combing his shiny black hair and putting sweet grease on it in front of the mirror. "Man, you are handsome!" the face in the mirror told him. My sisters were playing with Little Sergio when we pushed open the door.

I like to be in our house. The stove keeps it warm in the winter, and a big wire walks up the Hill to give light to the electric bulb. It shone now on the plates and spoons, waiting for their people to come to the table.

"It's ready!" Mama shouted. Nobody held back even a minute. Pop first, then Gramma, Roberto, Maria Helena, Maria Clara, Alberto, Carlos, Regina, and me held out our plates for Mama to smack a big spoonful of rice onto them. Then came a ladle of good-smelling beans, a few circles of greeny-yellow squash, and a dust of manioc flour.

As he does almost every night, Pop said, "Your Mama makes the best bean stew I ever ate."

And we all groaned, "Pop, we knew you were going to say that!"

"Well, your mother has the touch of an artist," said Pop, and Mama let just a little smile come.

"Hey!" Carlos remembered something. "They think they saw The Crocodile on our Hill! He robbed another bank. If I was him, I wouldn't walk around with all that money. It would show. I'd hide a little here, a little there.

Then, after the police went away, I'd go get it, and jump in my airplane. . . ."

"I don't want to hear you talk like that!" Mama shook her spoon at him. "Stealing and hiding money! That Crocodile is going to end up dead on the street! His poor Mama!"

Carlos went back to slupping up his food. I knew he was thinking where he would hide the money. "Mama! Carlos is so piggy! Look at him! He acts like he's digging a hole down to the street!"

"Mind your own plate, you're not eating at all," Mama scolded. It was true—my stomach was getting more and more scared. Suppose Teresinha dances so terrifically on Friday night that nobody looks at me?!

"Today, Little Sergio almost walked," Mama was saying. "He held out his arms to be taken, but Gramma and I said, 'Come on, little son, you can do it!' He was holding on to the chair and he let go. Yes, he did, but then he got scared and sat down so hard he started to cry."

Gramma said, "Remember when Maria Antonia was just that little? She was sitting on the concrete, watching the rehearsal. Everybody was dancing, all our family, the cousins, Aunt Sophia, myself. Maria Antonia was clapping her little hands and moving her body in time to the music. Then she tried to stand up and dance, but you see, she didn't walk yet. Naturally she fell down again. How she screamed! Her Poppa picked her up and danced her around in his arms. But no, that wasn't good enough.

35

She screamed and screamed because she wanted to dance by herself."

Mama and Pop nodded and smiled, remembering. Gramma always tells that story. But it's never boring— I was so cute, such a little fighter! Besides, it makes it truer, the secret thing.

"You're going to dance really well on Friday night." Maria Clara patted my head. "I think you'll be chosen to lead the kids' group."

This sister really knows who is a good dancer. Of all her friends, she's the fastest. Maria Clara could be the best on the Hill, but she loves to have a husband more than she loves Samba.

"I know where we're going to have the wedding picture taken. . . ." She's always thinking about her fiancé and the wedding. "It's a shop next to the street of the Flower Sellers." Mama and Pop have a wedding picture. It shows Mama in a white dress, looking very, very happy to be married. Her dress is so long and wide, there's almost no room for the husband. He's just a little Pop peeking out from behind it. That's the kind of picture Maria Clara wants.

"Don't waste those good beans now!" Mama scolded again. I was placing them around the plate so they'd look more eaten.

"I'll take hers," Carlos said.

"Here, greedy-guts." But I was glad to give him my supper. The worry had filled me up.

"Carlos's stomach is like a bank. The more he puts in it, the richer he feels," Pop said. He put down his little coffee cup. "So! Let's see how the costumes are coming."

Everybody picked up their dishes from the table, and Maria Clara wiped it clean—no greasy spots must get on the beautiful pink-and-green cloth!

Pop went behind the curtain to put on his shiny green suit with the pink stripe down each leg. He paraded out, fixing the green jacket's lapels, though they were already straight. (When he's dressed up like that, Pop looks bigger somehow.) "Hurray, Pop!" we all cheered. Pop took off his tall pink hat with the diamond buckle and bowed to us.

"Pop, you're Mr. Elegant!" Alberto said.

After we had looked at him enough, Gramma put the beautiful, slippery costume over my regular dress. By standing on the chair, I could see in the mirror. The tiny green bikini top with jewels all around the edge was adorable—but pushing out my chest didn't help. Nothing showed yet. Oh, well—I twirled the delicious raspberry skirt. Could it be me?! Yes, I know this kid with the too-big eyes and those skinny legs.

"Maria Antonia, what a nice-looking little girl you're getting to be, after all," Mama said. It wasn't true! Well, maybe it was a little true—if only I could always wear my costume!

Maria Helena's face showed in the mirror over my shoulder. She put her finger through one of those dumb

37

curls and pulled it, but not hard. "Such cute hair you've got." In the mirror I shook my head "no."

Would the Director, the important people, look at the ugly things about me, or would they see who I *really* am?

In my house we have cloth curtains hanging, to make a place for everybody. The boys sleep on one side, the girls on the other. Gramma has a special little room of curtains, and so do Mama and Poppa. I used to sleep with Gramma. She would whisper me stories about when she was a little girl, till Mama called out, "Gramma, you are as bad as Maria Antonia!"

Then Little Sergio came. Gramma said she didn't sleep much anyway; she would get up when he cried. So the baby sleeps with her, and I'm with Regina. Regina rolls my hair in fat pink curlers like she does her own. Then we go to sleep.

You surely can't get lonely in this house. But if you like to hide something, everybody knows where it is. Maria Helena has a box with a picture of chocolate cherries on it. Inside she keeps money she's saving for the Teacher Training Institute. We all know it's under Gramma's cushion on her rocking chair. But a robber wouldn't know that.

Late in the afternoon, I came from practicing some hard new steps with the Children's Group. No one was home yet. Flopping on Gramma's bed, I began talking with this other person—it's really me, of course, but I like to hear her talk. *See how well you picked up those fast steps, honey. You gave Teresinha the dust off your feet!* I grinned. "I really did, didn't I?" I waited for more nice things about me. But the door opened, and Maria Clara and Maria Helena came in talking very fast.

They couldn't see me behind Gramma's curtain. I pretended I wasn't listening, but you want to know what the big girls talk about. And after all, I was here first.

"No, it's too late, I have decided," Maria Helena said. "I can't possibly save enough money this year for the teacher training. I couldn't last year, and that's how it's always going to be. I just better get married or do laundering in the street."

"Wait," Maria Clara told her, "I can give you some

41

Squadron Line Media Center
Simsbury, Connecticut

money after Eduardo and I get married. And Mama and Pop will too. They want you to be a teacher. They'd be really proud of you—'Madame Professor Maria Helena dos Santos'!"

"Ahhh! Boo-boo-ooo!"

I sat up. It was Maria Helena. I wished she wouldn't cry. It makes me too sad.

"What's the use? I never should have had such ideas." More crying. "It's better if you are what you are and don't try to be something else." Sniff. Sniff.

"Be calm, be calm. I'll help, and Regina. The boys will help."

But I knew and Maria Clara did too—the big boys had girl friends and wanted to get married. They needed every penny for the rings and the dresses. And their girl friends wouldn't get married without those things.

"How much is still needed for the registration?"

"10,000* cruzeiros, and there's only one week to sign up!"

"Don't be so excited! Something will happen. Wipe your eyes and get ready for the meeting. You'll see, something good will happen."

What could happen to bring money if there is no money? I wondered. It's terribly sad, but what could I do? The house was filling up. I slipped off Gramma's bed and out from behind the curtains. Nobody even saw me.

_____

*Approximately $20.00

Roberto and Pop spoke seriously about the meeting tonight. "I am worried," Roberto said. "That Fernando Freitas tries to make everybody do what he wants."

"Well," Pop said, "I don't think he can do that. Our people are not puppets."

"But you don't see the most important thing, Poppa!" Roberto was waving his hands and walking back and forth. "The thing he is trying to do is change Samba itself! He is trying to make Carnival a show for the tourists! He wants to change the tradition!"

I don't see what Roberto gets so excited about. Samba is Samba. You are born with it in you, and you just do it. No one can change that. Alberto patted his shoulder. "Don't worry, Roberto. I am traditional—and still, when the tourists see how superb I look in my green satin trousers and pink jacket, they'll cheer."

The top of Nilton's head and his eyes showed at the window. "Pssst! Maria Antonia! Let's go early." Before Mama could notice, I was out the door and trotting down the path with Nilton.

We ducked under everybody's arms and pushed into the meeting hall with Louisa and John from the Northeast and Hambone. That Teresinha was there, of course, trying to get me to look at her. But I wouldn't! People should stay where they belong and not move all the way from Bahia just so they can spoil everything for other people.

"Maria Antonia!" Louisa was pushing something in

43

my face. "Look at all I got on the Avenue of Our Lady of Copacabana for only 100 cruzeiros! This big diamond ring and purple lipstick and an eyebrow pencil, because I'm gonna pull out my eyebrows and draw them on again with the pencil."

"You look good in that color lipstick," I told her. "You look fifteen." Louisa's always trying to look old, so she likes me to say that.

When we all squeezed up in front, we saw that Mr. Fernando Freitas, the Director of Choreography, was talking. He's the one Roberto worries about. His hair is waved in little rows, and I guess he is handsome. But I don't like him. His eyes don't see even somebody like Pop. He only talks to the important people. I don't mean my Pop isn't important! He is the most important man I know! But Pop doesn't talk a lot, and he doesn't *act* important.

"I have choreographed new parts," Mr. Freitas said, "for fifteen slaves who will whirl around the Queen, fall on their faces, and crawl before her."

Some people turned to their neighbors and said, "What a clever new idea! The other Samba Schools won't have anything like that."

But Poppa suddenly jumped up and cried, "No one should be forced to take the part of a slave! We Samba dancers of The Hill of the Cashew Tree will gladly be citizens who admire our Queen. But crawling slaves, never!"

Cheers flew up to the roof. Nilton and I clapped till our hands stung. "I never knew Poppa could make a speech like that!"

"Your Pop doesn't talk much, but when he does, he's really smart."

Maria Helena was clapping too, but her face was sad. She wants to be a teacher so much. I know just how it feels. But what I'm going to be doesn't need money; you can't buy the job of Queen.

Amarilda "Lock on the Pocketbook" waved her hand in the face of the President, who was also Director of Rehearsals. "Your honor, I want to say that it would perhaps be a good idea if the costumes of the shepherdesses were made simpler this year. Less cloth would result in faster movement. I also suggest that we not use the high white wigs, which are hot and may slip down."

A big roar from the whole room, "No! No!" The President held up his hand.

"We are poor. Yes, we are poor." Silence. "But we must show the City, the world, that we are Kings and Queens in the Country of Samba." Cheers! "Some may say, 'We Brazilians are a republic. Even a democracy.' And we are. Some may say, 'We have no Kings and Queens.' But I say, 'Samba is the beating heart of Brazil and we are its defenders. Kings and Queens must look like Kings and Queens. With our satins, our jewels, our wigs, everyone is royal!' "

People beat on their chairs and stamped the floor. "Bravo! Bravo!"

Now the Director of Harmony stood up. "I agree with the Honorable President. But I also agree with . . ."

I groaned, "Let's get out of here." Nilton nodded.

Outside, we headed for Hungry Joe's mango tree. Mama says, "Now don't go climbing trees. The boys might see your panties." But who cares about such silly things? I don't, and Nilton doesn't either.

It's nice sitting in a tree at night. Nobody knew we were there except Hungry Joe's chicken, Sylvia. She moved over on her branch, giving us the bad eye. People passed under, dogs ran by. On our faces the moon made dark leaf-shadows. Our secret eyes looked through the branches. "Nilton," I whispered, "we are two leopards waiting in a tree by the Amazon. . . ."

I was thinking, to jump down on Teresinha, when Nilton said, "Come on, the meeting is over."

We tumbled out of the tree to get home before Mama and Pop. Behind Lindomar's store, back where Louisa lives, there is a kids' path. Grown-ups don't go there; it's too steep and narrow. But goats and pigs do, and that's how I slipped on you know what! I bumped Nilton, who was ahead of me, and we both went crashing down the hillside into an old garbage hole with bushes growing over it.

"I couldn't help it, Nilton!" I was explaining when he sat up, brushing off ashes and fruit peels.

46

"Never mind. What are those papers in your hair?"

Putting up my hand I felt something like—bus tickets? No! A 100-cruzeiro bill was caught in my ponytail! "Nilton! There are cruzeiros all over here! Look! In the garbage, all over! Oh, Nilton, we're rich!"

"Rich? I don't know. Let's count." We crawled all over, picking up money and calling out, "50 cruzeiros!" "100!"

When there was no more to find, Nilton said, "20,000 cruzeiros,* and I think I know whose it is."

"It's ours!" I cried. "We found it!"

"Yes, but I think it was put here by The Crocodile."

"The bandit? Yow! Will he come for it?! Let's get away from here!"

"He can't come for it. He's in jail. Remember when the police chased him from Isabella's house, over there? He must have run here and buried the money."

"Do we have to give it back?"

"How could we go to the jail and give it to him? It's ours; 10,000 for you, 10,000 for me. Come on." Nilton pulled me up out of the hole and we climbed to the path.

Money kept spilling from my hands. "What will we do, now that we're rich?"

"We're not so rich. Put your money in your pocket where it's safe. Me, I'm going to buy a bus ticket to Bahia, to look for my father."

"Don't go away, Nilton!" I almost said it. But he wouldn't

---

*Approximately $40.00

47

know where to look in Bahia. So it's all right, he'll never go.

Ooh, the dress I could buy! The red shoes with busy little heels that went "tack—tack" on the floor, like my sisters'. I might even get one of those long pieces of hair to stick in my own! It would go straight like water down my back. I'd be 100 times prettier than Teresinha!

"Here's your house, Maria Antonia," Nilton said, or I might have gone by it.

The door opened and Mama called out, "Here she is!" Mama pulled me in the house and shut the door. "Everybody's asleep already! Look at you! Covered with dirt!"

Pop said, "It's not good for a little girl to be out late in the night. Something bad could happen."

Bad?! I almost said, "Good things can happen too." But it was better to surprise them. After I got my dress and my shoes and my beautiful straight hair, everybody would get a nice present.

Jumping in bed, I was spending my money. I might buy a blue dress with red shoes, or a red dress with slippery, shiny black shoes, like Alberto has. And the long tail of hair—would I look good in brown or a reddish kind? That hair is expensive. But it's real nylon, so it would last probably all my life. Presents for everybody would cost a lot too. Maybe more than I had!

Maria Helena sighed a long sigh, like you do when you can't cry anymore.

Should I? Should I? What if I just got shoes and the

49

reddish hair? Or no shoes and just the hair? I sat up and put my feet over the edge of the bed. I reached for my dress on its nail. It was hard not to bump into the breathing hills of people on the way to Gramma's chair. Under the cushion, it was right there, the box with cherries on it. How easy to open. . . . Maybe money likes to be with more money. Mine slipped right into the box.

I got in bed and snuggled my backside against Regina's. She turned and put her arm around me, and that made me feel a little better. We slept that way.

Maria Helena woke us all with her screams.

"What is it?!" "What's happened?!"

She held out her box.

"She's been robbed! Oh, Saints in Heaven!" Mama put her hand to her heart.

"No, no!" Maria Helena laughed and wept at the same time. "My money is here. But there's 20,000 cruzeiros now!"

"Who can explain this?" Poppa looked around at us. I was keeping quiet, it was such a good joke. But I couldn't stop smiling. "Maria Antonia, what do you know about this?"

"Well, Poppa, Nilton and I found 20,000 cruzeiros in the old garbage hole. We think it must be The Crocodile's."

"The Crocodile's! He'll come back for it! We're in danger!" Mama cried.

"No—he's going to jail for twenty-five years." Alberto calmed her.

"We each took half," I went on.

"And you gave it to your sister. What a fine girl you are!" Poppa looked so proud of me.

"Now you can go to the teacher's school," I told Maria Helena.

And Mama said, "That's the way sisters should be to each other."

"But first," Poppa said, "we must see if someone is waiting for the 10,000 cruzeiros to be returned."

"Poppa," Alberto told him, "you can't go to Bahia and Pernambuco and Minas and give it back. The Crocodile took over three million cruzeiros."

Carlos was dancing up and down. "Don't do it, Poppa! Those banks have all that money. We need some!"

"But Poppa! . . ." I started and stopped. It was no use. I knew how Poppa is—he is the most terribly honest person I ever saw.

Poppa said, "We have to try to return it. Suppose it

was Mama's pocketbook that was found? Wouldn't we want somebody to return it to her? I'll go to the *Jornal do Brasil* and ask them what to do. They'll know." And he went right away.

Mama scrubbed her clean pots again. Maria Helena and Maria Clara prayed the whole time, very fast. Maybe if God heard so many prayers he would say, "Stop pestering me! Here, here is what you want!" Sitting on the steps, I waited. "The hours must be stuck," I thought.

Suddenly, Poppa was back, smiling! "Tell us, Poppa, tell us!"

"Well, I went into those glass doors that go around and push you in the back. Then, I didn't know what to do, but an important lady with her hair on top of her head like a mountain, like a Sugar-Loaf Mountain, was sitting there. She's the one who says, 'You can go in. You must stay out.' 'What do you want?' she asked me. I told her the whole story. 'Don't bother to go in,' she said. 'I can tell you that's such a pitiful little bit of money! They'll laugh. Why we had a man in Sunday's paper that found a fifty-million-cruzeiro emerald necklace in his taxi. Now, that's a story! Go home with your pennies, my dear fellow, and buy your kiddies some candy.' So, our good, kind Maria Antonia can give her sister the money." Mama and the girls were all crying.

The brothers roughed my hair and told me, "You're a

good kid, Maria Antonia." Gramma winked and nodded. Her smile said, "I knew it was Maria Antonia who did that."

Maria Helena hugged me. "When I am a teacher, I will pay you back three times as much." But that was a long time away from now.

Sitting on the steps after breakfast, I dreamed how I would have looked: the tight red dress with satin ruffles, the high heels that make you walk like you are eighteen years old. "Stop thinking about it!" I ordered myself and went inside to watch Roberto play his guitar. He and Alberto were home from work today.

Roberto strummed softly. He bent his dark head to hear what the guitar was telling him. Sometimes he sang to himself, whispering the words. Roberto was composing a Samba song for our school. Alberto was looking hard at all his clothes, like he was getting ready for something. They took up the most space on the clothesline that went across the room, holding everybody's good dresses and shirts.

"What do you think of this, Alberto?" Strum, strum.

"Go, go my heart.
Go to the heart
That smiles for me.
We'll meet at Carnival."

Strum, strum, strum.

"Well . . . it sounds a little like something I already

heard. But there are fine parts in it." Alberto held a yellow-and-green Hawaiian shirt under his chin, gazed at the mirror, and shook his head.

I leaned against Gramma's rocker. "What is it, dear little girl?"

"Tell me a story, won't you, Gramma?" She was sewing a hole in Carlos's sneaker, where his toe always comes through from kicking the soccer ball. (Gramma wasn't such a good fixer, but we would *never* tell her.)

Still pushing the needle through the old gray sneaker, Gramma began. "This is the story of how a girl got changed into a guinea pig, and it's true. I saw that girl after she was changed back again. Her nose still moved up and down like a guinea pig's. She was an Indian girl of the Amazon. Her father was the chief. This girl was pretty and she was proud of that. She told the other girls, 'Take care and don't annoy me because I am the chief's daughter.' Then one day the animals came out of the jungle. There was a green sliding snake with amethyst eyes, and a leopard with real solid gold spots. They said to her, 'You must come with us and be our maid because you are too proud.' And they turned her into a guinea pig. Yes, they did. For seven years she had to wait on them. Then one day her father was in the jungle and they were going to eat him! The guinea-pig girl jumped in the front and said, 'Don't eat him! Eat me!' So they told her, 'Now you are not proud anymore, and you love your father, so you can be a girl again.' "

"That's a good story, Gramma. I don't think it can be true."

"Oh, it is! It is!"

"Well, the sliding green snake and the leopard are nice parts anyhow," I thought.

Roberto tried another song. "Listen to this!

"O Hill of Samba!
Hill of Song!
Only one true one for me
Is The Hill of the Cashew Tree."

He had to hurry to make some parts fit in. Roberto is trying so hard to be a composer.

"Why don't you take another theme, something new, something fresh?" Alberto told him. Roberto looked disappointed. Then he went back to his guitar, waiting for the idea to come.

"Maria Antonia! I heard you had all that money and you gave it away! Why did you do that? Are you crazy or something?" Louisa rushed in the door.

I took her by the elbow out to the steps. "Shhh! Roberto is composing." Then I said, "Maria Helena needed to go to the teacher's school. I couldn't keep it."

"But you could have bought so much good stuff! I saw this picture of Roberto Antonio! It's all velvet and they painted his picture on it, and you could hang it on the wall because it's big as a rug. You could have bought that!" Roberto Antonio is her lovey-boy singing star on T.V.

"Louisa, I wouldn't do that. He's *your* sweetheart. Let's practice."

I jumped down, right into a fast turn and lots of double-quick steps. Louisa started dancing and singing, "Lei! Lei! La! La! Hey! Look at me!" I kicked my rubber sandals in the air. Louisa did too. "Lei! Lei! La! La!"

We were dancing and laughing so much, Roberto came to the door with his guitar.

For a while he watched. Then he sat on the step and began to play and sing:

"Children of Samba,
  Birds of Happiness,
  Do you know
  How happy you make us?"

"What a beautiful Samba, Roberto!" "Did you just compose it?" "Oh, it's so good!" Louisa and I told him.

Alberto came out. "You should bring it to Zeca's right away."

"Do you really think so, Alberto?"

Alberto threw down his armful of shirts and neckties. He grabbed Roberto and his guitar and pushed him up the Hill toward Zeca's. Louisa and I ran after them.

When we came there, Zeca was sitting on his porch having beers with his friends. Their guitars and man-

57

dolins and flutes were laid down by their chairs. Alberto pushed our brother forward.

"Here, Mr. Zeca, President of the Composers, is another member for your group. You'll see! Play your new Samba for them, Roberto. Go ahead."

And Roberto did play. The composers leaned forward. They smiled and picked up their instruments. "Children of Samba," they played and sang too. When they finished, Zeca put his arm around Roberto.

"Good, very good, young man. We elect you right now into our group." Roberto backed away, too pleased to say anything.

Going back, Louisa and I ran along looking up at him. "You're better than a movie star!" I told him.

"Almost as good as Roberto Antonio!" Louisa said.

Alberto stopped. "I have something to tell you." He looked unhappy suddenly. "My boss offered me a better job. I'd be the traveling salesman for the company. It would be necessary for me to go to Belo Horizonte, Bahia, many places, and show the new line of plastic dishes. I'd wear a three-piece suit, a thin-striped gray one, I think, and a watch, to look good for the company, you know. I'd stay in hotels and take a drink in the bar in the evenings."

Mama would be upset to have one of her children so far away, I knew!

"But you would be here for Carnival and the Night on the Avenue, wouldn't you?" Roberto asked.

58

"No." Alberto looked down.

"But who would take your part in the story?"

"Well, I guess any handsome fellow could."

"I can't say you shouldn't take the job. It means much more money and the three-piece striped suit and watch. You'd be very happy, I suppose."

"I suppose I would. But I'm telling my boss 'No!' When I heard your Samba, I just couldn't do it! I couldn't leave the Hill and our Samba School. I was a child of Samba too, you know."

Louisa and I squealed and hugged each other. Roberto shook Alberto's hand. Alberto shook Roberto's. They just kept shaking hands and looking at each other.

It was hot! Even on top of our Hill, where breezes are always chasing each other out of the sky. You could see the heat down in the City, hanging over it like a white curtain. Behind the curtain, the apartments looked all wavy and the streets were bending.

Louisa sat with her legs straight out, admiring the red polish on her toenails. "Heat is good at Carnival, that's why they have it. It makes you dance better."

"Yeah," John from the Northeast said, lying on his back. "Your legs bend more and you can go faster."

I flopped down next to Louisa and fanned myself with the hanky Mama made me carry. "The sweat is like oil running all over you and that's good for dancing Samba," I said. "Where's Nilton?"

"Maybe in the City, maybe in the woods," John said.

More kids came when they finished working or going to Lindomar's for their mothers. Fat Fernando, Laurita, and her boyfriend, Aldo, and Damon "The Worrier." Then Gabriel came. He's got scribbled curls, like I used to draw on people in first grade—when I went to school, that is.

Where was Nilton?! He's never here, always some-place else! He makes me mad. "Let's bet," I said. Every kid had "money" in a cloth bag, pieces of broken dishes or glass. The ones with flowers or stripes are worth a lot, and we spent a lot of time rubbing off the sharp edges. Holding up a flower one, I said, "I'll bet that 'Say, Sweet Little Girl' is going to win at the Festival of Popular Music."

Aldo held up the blue edge of a dish. " 'My Tears Are Yours' is gonna win!" We smacked palms. The bet was on.

"Maria Antonia! Let's you and me bet who's going to marry us!" Louisa likes to say that this one is in love with her, and that this one tried to kiss her. I don't have to marry anybody to be Queen. Still, I held up a plain "money."

"Here, this says that Hector is going to marry you."

61

Hector is twenty years old and Louisa is crazy for him.

She was so happy, she screamed, "Oh, you're awful, Maria Antonia!"

"But we have to wait five years for this bet," I told her. She giggled and pushed me in the chest.

Hambone got bored with betting. "Damon," he said, and I could tell he was going to tease, "Damon, it's starting right now!" (Damon has these funny ideas; he thinks the world is going to turn into plastic and there will be nothing you can eat. That's why we call him "The Worrier.") "Oh! Oh! It's turning into plastic!"

"Stop that, Hambone! He'll believe you, poor thing." I made a fist. Hambone laughed, but he knew I would punch him.

To show how cool he was, Hambone took out a matchbox and tapped on it. John took his tambourine from where he kept it on his belt, and they started making Samba music together. Gabriel ran into his house for his mother's frying pan and beat on it with a big spoon, his curls shaking with each smack. Aldo put pebbles in a tin can and rattled them. Fat Fernando took his comb and scraped a stick back and forth across the top.

Louisa jumped up and flipping her skirt yelled, "Wow! I'm gonna 'Shake and Bake'!" And she began dancing with her head wagging, her elbows poking the air, and her sharp knees going every which way.

Everybody laughed and cheered, "Hey, Louisa!" John from the Northeast threw his tambourine in the air, did a somersault, and caught it! Sebastian was right next to him, dancing on his hands.

"Hey, John!"

"Hey, Sebastian, man!"

When Louisa fell down giggling, Laurita took her place. "Talk to me!" She snapped her fingers for someone to join her, and I did. I was so good! Everybody stopped to watch.

"Go my beauties, go!" shouted Hambone, just like the Director. Grown-ups going by laughed and nodded, and I bent my head, smiling like a real Queen, like the Flag Bearer.

Suddenly, "Baaa!" A black-and-white hairy monster butted right into the middle of us! It was Aristotle with a screaming tail of little kids. "We're trying to catch him! He got away!" They were yelling and throwing stones at that poor goat, so he'd never stop.

"You're scaring him!" I started after them. Over rocks, into bushes, through Alberto Nascimento's front door and out the back, to the edge of the cliff, and . . . no more Aristotle!

I pushed my way by the little kids. They were afraid to look, and so was I. But there wasn't any white splash in the green water way below; there wasn't any broken black-and-white "toy" on the beach, like a dog I saw after the bus ran over it.

"Baaa!" In a thorny bush partway down, Aristotle was hanging by his long hair.

Hambone and Louisa came and leaned over. "I don't want to see him if he's dead!" screamed Louisa.

"Should I get Nilton's uncle?" Hambone stared at me.

"Get anybody!" I pushed them toward the houses and people. Then I fell on my stomach, with eyes tight on Aristotle. The other little kids had run away, but Hambone's smallest sister, Amelia, was crying and wiping her nose on my dress.

"I didn't mean it! My mother's gonna hit me!"

The bush was pulling out—only a few hairy-spider roots hung on to the cliff. "Oh, Aristotle, you're going to be dead!" Nilton's uncle would say it was Nilton's fault for not tying Aristotle better! He would beat him with big, hard fists! Digging in my nails and toes, I let myself over the edge. Loose rocks and pebbles fell slowly down to the bottomless ocean. I didn't dare to look. The closer I came, the more that silly animal kicked.

"Stop it, Aristotle!" I threw my arms around him and held on to the cliff with my shoulders, with my nose, with anything! "Stop, you crazy goat, or I'll let you fall!" Aristotle's dumb yellow eyes looked into mine. "You'll help me, won't you, Maria Antonia?!" The thorn bush had two more roots to go. Someone must be coming. Could I hold on?!

"Maria Antonia! Catch this!" A rope hit my head and I looked up. Nilton's scared eyes and wild hair showed over the edge. Maybe because Aristotle knew Nilton was there, he stopped fighting. Now I could tie the rope around

64

him, under his front feet. Nilton pulled. Aristotle began to rise. I scratched my way up till I could reach Nilton's hand, and he yanked me onto the safe earth at the top. Right away I began moving all the parts I need for dancing. Toes, ankles, knees—ALL OKAY! and Gramma's curing medicine would fix the scratches.

Nilton bent over me. "Are you hurt, Maria Antonia?"

"No, but I could have been!" Now that it was over, I was getting mad. "Why don't you keep that smelly goat tied up? I might have died and missed the Night on the Avenue!"

"It wasn't me," Nilton said. "Rinaldo dared Amelia to let him go. If Aristotle got killed, my uncle would try to beat me and I wouldn't let him. I'd have to go away— to Bahia, maybe."

I looked away and petted Aristotle's rough head between his horns. Forgetting how scared he was, he began to eat my dress.

"Okay, okay," I said.

It was getting closer to Friday rehearsal. The Director might choose Teresinha. If only she'd get carried away by a giant bird!

"Hey, look what I've got! It's for you, on account of Aristotle!" Nilton was coming up the path, waving two pink pieces of paper.

I took them and handed them back. "What does it say? What good are they anyway?!" (Nervous! Why was I so nervous all the time now? *Well, honey, of course you're nervous. It's terrible what that Teresinha is trying to do to you!*)

Nilton was saying, "These are tickets. A big, red-in-the-face tourist lady was outside the Museum and the tickets blew out of her hand. She whistled like a guinea pig for her husband to catch them, but the wind wanted me to have those tickets." I had to smile at the funny pictures Nilton made about people. "The man let her in anyhow. So I'm going to take you to the Museum."

That building is far away from the Hill, where the ferry bustles out of its house to cross the harbor. Nilton goes there a lot with his wagon, picking up the good stuff that gets thrown in the street.

"It's far, Nilton."

"There are pictures there, Maria Antonia. Pictures of Queens."

He knows I am interested in Queens, the Queens of Samba, the Queen of England—I saw her in the newspaper, but they didn't say if she was a good dancer—fairy-tale Queens. I love to know about all the other Queens. Maybe I should go with Nilton. The worry running alongside me like a little dog might stay here on the Hill. "Okay. But let's go by the way where you see the big ships coming to Rio." That way was far from the pump where Mama was washing clothes and gabbing to her friends.

When we came to the lookout place, we could see to the end of the world. "Don't the boats look like little bugs crawling on a big slippery floor?"

"Those boats are bigger than an apartment building

68

lying down flat," Nilton said. But that was hard to believe. "Let's go. It's a long way." Nilton jumped down to the path with me following.

We came to Zeca's house—he is always having a party. The composers were singing and playing their new Sambas and the old ones that they loved. A flute stayed in the air like a silver bird. "Ahhh, what longing I have for Emilia! Ahhh, what coffee she made, that girl!"

Down we came onto the big street where a yellow bus was just grunting up to the bus stop. "Quick!" Nilton swung me up the step and put money in the glass box. The bus groaned forward, sitting us down hard in the seats.

"This bus is cranky, like the driver," I whispered to Nilton. "My Pop always says something when you get on his bus, like 'it's sure hot today.' "

"You've got a good Pop," Nilton said. He bent to pick up a cigarette from under the seat and stuck it behind his ear to sell later.

We held on tight to the seats in front of us and gazed at every store that went by. "ONLY TODAY! THE CHEAPEST SUITS IN RIO!" "SALE!" "SALE!" "NOBODY BEATS OUR PRICES!" Then, little mountains of sweet-smelling buns and pretty sugared cakes, right out in front.

"Bakeries are best," I said to Nilton. "I'm going to run in and grab those with the red jelly and chocolate sprinkles. And if the man tries to stop me, I'll do judo on him. 'Hai! Eeae!' "

69

"You don't need judo. I'll buy some for you," Nilton said, "but I prefer the pink iced kind with the almond sitting on top." We could really "taste" the little cakes. Then we "tried" the crackling rolls like fat cigars and the soft, round ones called "Babys' Bottoms." "Enough! I'm full," Nilton said, petting his stomach, and I burped a fake burp. The people in the bus turned around. We poked each other and grinned.

Now downtown was tall around us. The buildings were too high to see the tops. Little stores turned into marble and glass boxes, so people couldn't touch the jewels and cameras and T.V.s. Many buses were roaring onto the avenue, and cars and taxis pushed into any space between them.

"Come on, we get off here!" and Nilton pulled me down the steps before the cranky bus could pinch us in its doors.

We stood on the sidewalk, two little ants in a city full of big ants. "Aiii! How could anyone know all these people, Nilton?"

"You don't have to." Nilton grabbed my hand and started across. I held on to him, trying not to look. But Nilton knew how to do this and we came safely to the other curb. "We have to go toward the harbor, there." He pointed with his chin down the enormous street, between the giant buildings. One shouted "I AM THE BANK OF GUANABARA!" another "YOU MUST DRINK COCA-COLA!" and still another "FORD IS THE BEST!" At the end

70

of the avenue was the same water we saw from our Hill.

On the corner where we stood was a Kibon Man, but not the one who came to the bottom of The Cashew Tree. This was a joking man who called to Nilton, "Buy your girl friend a Vanilla Cup, a Caramel Crunch, a Pineapple Surprise." It was nice that somebody not from our Hill knew Nilton was my boyfriend. Nilton was looking in his pocket for money. He bought a double orange Frostie with two sticks. Then he broke it in half and gave one stick to me.

We were pulling out the sweet, cold orange color with our mouths, watching what other people bought: a Swiss Mountain with chocolate dripping down a vanilla peak and a little flat wooden spoon to eat it with—200 cruzeiros! Raspberry Delight, red as sunset—250! A Dream of Chocolate floating in a fudgy pool—265 cruzeiros! Nilton threw down his stick. "Come on."

He trotted me onto little side streets that ran off the great avenue. On some they sold only flowers, on others, only baskets. On every street a man would run alongside you, talking very fast, trying to sell a lottery ticket or a key chain with a cute little doll on it.

It was good that I came—I might get in trouble with Mama for not telling her I was going to the Museum. But, at least I wouldn't have to think about Teresinha.

There it was—the Museum! It had a long, long white porch with lots of posts curved at the top, and pink walls. Baby angels were playing with fruits and ribbons around all the windows and doors.

"It looks like it's in an old-fashioned time. It's nicer than regular buildings."

Nilton wasn't listening. He was making up his mind. Then he went to the ticket man in his little cage and held out the crumpled pink papers.

The man didn't stop scratching his pen along in front of him. Nilton held out the tickets. Pushing his glasses on top of his bald head—it had three long hairs smoothed across it—the man stared at Nilton. He knows we didn't buy them. He's not going to let us in! Suddenly, a smile slid from the top of the ticket man's shiny head down onto his face. "Go, go," he said, waving us into the Museum.

We went in slowly to the biggest room in the world! And we could see another after that! To look at the ceiling, we had to put our heads way back, and a quiet came down from there so that we began to whisper. White stone people stood on little tables, pointing at nothing in the air. I moved closer to Nilton. Only stone men and ladies could live in this too-quiet place without any breeze.

"Where are the Queens, Nilton?"

"That's a King over there. See his crown on the table next to him?" Nilton pointed to an enormous dark picture with real gold all around it. We stood under it, gazing up at the King's soft white velvet stomach and shiny blue cape. His round white legs and black slippers looked like a lady's. Gold stars and medals pushed each other for space on his chest. And he looked very seriously into some bushes on the side.

"Nilton," I whispered, "read the sign."

"It says, 'King John VI,' but I don't think he's much of a King. He looks like he's got a plum stuck in both his cheeks. That one there is better—'The Emperor Dom Pedro I.' " This Emperor had a cute mustache and nice brown eyes.

"But where are the Queens?" We wandered further, peeking into more rooms with dusty glass cases and more big dark pictures and more statues, very white in the gray air. Then we saw them, looking down at us from under diamond crowns and fountains of feathers—the Queens!

"The Archduchess Leopoldina, Queen Carlota, Princess Amelia," Nilton read out their names.

"They sound pretty, Nilton, but I just have to say it—they're kind of funny-looking, poor things. Look, this Archduchess is letting her chin slide into her neck. This Queen puts out her chin like a shovel, and Princess Amelia didn't get any chin." Not all the silk clothes with jewels stuck on everywhere could make them smile either.

I thought of how our Queen of the Samba, Wilma, smiled when she danced. When she went down to work in the City in her neat dark skirt and white blouse, she smiled too. Even when she was dusting her house with a clean cloth around her hair, she was smiling.

"Well, but do you like them?" Nilton asked.

So he wouldn't be disappointed, I answered, "My sisters aren't going to believe all the clothes and jewels on these Queens!"

"Wait till you see this," Nilton said. "There's a garden and a carriage that horses used to pull." I followed him out a side door into the garden. Banana trees waved their green fans, and a little fountain was talking into a stone basin. How blue the sky was, and how many cool breezes there were outside the Museum!

74

"Isn't this neat?" Nilton circled around a shiny box with wheels and two long poles. It was really a little room to ride in, with windows and red velvet cushions, and even curtains with gold drips. Gold leaves and crowns were stuck on the doors, and there was a gold step for the King and Queen to put their feet on when they got in and out. I touched my finger to the side—it was smooth as black water.

Screamy parrot voices made us jump. Two ladies in tight dresses with little gold watches on their wrists came into the garden. They had to hold on to their husbands or they'd have fallen off their high, pointy heels. When they saw us, they stopped talking. Their stiff, puffed-up hair seemed to puff higher. Their little eyes said, "*You* don't belong here." I looked at Nilton. He was looking carefully at the carriage wheels. When he was done, he said, "I think we should go to our homes now, Maria Antonia." He said it just like someone in the movies!

I looked at "a little gold watch" on my wrist. "Yes, it's time, my dear." And we strolled past the ladies holding on to their husbands and staring.

We went out of the gate to the sidewalk. Then we had to stuff our hands in our mouths to stop laughing. Those ladies looked so funny!

Suddenly, I wasn't laughing anymore. Across the street, there she was,Teresinha and her mother! "She's following me, Nilton!"

"She's not following you. Why should she be following

you? She's just shopping with her mother." Nilton shook his head.

It was true. Her mother had two big shopping bags.

"Let's go home, Nilton. Mama is going to be mad because I didn't tell her I was going."

I was lost, but Nilton hurried me along till we came to the bus stop. It was the end of work for the downtown people, so a long line was waiting. Street lamps went on along the purple evening streets. In the jeweler's windows, colored stones burned green and lavender in circles of gold.

When the bus came, there were no empty seats. We got in the long worm of people moving on and pressing tight together. Nobody could fall even though the bus started with a crazy jerk. Our eyes were the only things we could move, so we gazed at all the riders. Men and women tried to sleep standing up, they were so tired from their work. Girl friends giggled about their boyfriends who were taking them to Carnival. One girl, like my sisters, swung her long, ripply hair and laughed, "I'm going to dance till my boyfriend drops on the floor!" "And then you'll get another one," her friends teased.

I always watch the bunches of schoolgirls—but I don't let them see me watching. They wear nice ironed white blouses and dark blue pleated skirts rolled up short so their legs can show. I think they unroll them when they get to school. They hug loads of books in their arms and they go to school every day.

I used to go to school, but I stayed out all the time to practice my dancing. Mama and Pop got tired of yelling at me, "Go to school!" School is too much sitting. Anyhow, why should I go if it just makes me feel dumb? Those girls are smart, but can they dance as good as me? Do they love Carnival like I do?

On and on the tired bus groaned. When three people squeezed off, four squeezed on. The faces of the Queens dreamed in my head, mixed up with Teresinha's. I punched her in the face and she turned into the Princess Amelia! I was almost asleep, but Nilton was pulling my arm. "We're here, Maria Antonia! Get off, quick!" And we were in the street looking up at our Hill. It was dark as black paper, with prickles of light scratched through. No mothers were at the pump. They were fixing supper for the fathers coming slowly up the Hill and for children who had gone far and come home safely.

"Next time I'll tell Mama where I'm going," I promised myself. "So long, Nilton. That was really a good Museum." I hurried up the path. And there it was, just like a little dog that wants to go everywhere you do—the worry "Is it Teresinha? Is it me? Who is going to be chosen?"

We were sitting on the wood steps of our house after supper—we always do that—Pop, Mama, Gramma holding Little Sergio, and me. Of course, my big brothers and sisters were with their girl friends and boyfriends. Carlos, the pest, was bouncing his soccer ball from his heel to his toe to his shoulder to his head. "Stop for a minute with that ball!" Pop and Mama begged. But they are really proud of him. We're sure when he grows up we'll all go to see him in the Stadium and roar when he makes the goal. (He is still a pest.)

It makes you dreamy, watching the night coming up

out of the sea. Darker and darker the sea gets. Higher and higher it comes up, till it covers the City and still it keeps coming. And the cars and the lit-up apartments are swimming under the soft, dark sea. . . .

"Heyyy!" Nilton and all the kids jumped out from around the back of the house. "Maria Antonia! Come on! We're gonna fool around!"

"Can I, Mama?"

She looked like "NO," but she said, "Well—all right. Don't be wild now."

Rattling fences, jumping from rocks, our gang moved down the Hill.

"Maria Antonia," Louisa said, "my cousin is home from the City for vacation. She's *so* cute, and she's got gorgeous clothes."

"She's a teacher, isn't she?"

"Yeah, that's the best job. You always wear a real nice dress, and you sit in the front of the room and tell the kids, 'Here, study this stuff.' Then you look in the mirror from your purse and touch your hair with your fingernails, all pink." Louisa acted as if she was holding a small mirror and patted around her tight, little pigtail. "I'm gonna be a teacher."

I didn't say what job I was going to have because Queen of the Samba is not a job. It's a special, wonderful thing that you just *are*.

Everybody began saying what was the best job. John from the Northeast's father worked in a big house on a

79

long avenue. They gave him the food on the plates after their parties. John said, "That's the job for me, being a waiter. You get shrimps, meat pies, everything!"

"The best job is my uncle's!" Hambone said. "He's the guy that sits in the cage and takes the money in the bank."

"Yeah, but he doesn't *get* the money."

"That's all right. He can touch it." Every day we'd see Hambone's uncle going down the Hill with a plastic leather briefcase. Only his lunch was inside, we all knew. Still, he looked important.

"Not me. I'm not going to have a job in a bank and go in the City every day with a briefcase," Nilton said.

"What are you going to do, Nilton?"

He thought for a minute—"I'm going wherever I want to; maybe I'll take some pretty things to sell. Then I'll go off again, wherever I want to go."

"That's not a job!" John shook his head.

"Your kids want to have clothes and everything. You can't do that!" Hambone shouted.

Nilton just smiled. He knew that's what he was going to do anyway.

We were getting bored.

"Hey, Nilton! Remember when you took the fishing pole and stuck it in his room and caught Ze Pereira's false teeth? He didn't even wake up! That was great!"

John from the Northeast slapped Nilton on the back.

I wanted to keep the teeth and drop them in somebody's bean stew, but Nilton put them back by Ze's bed. "We've got to do something wild like that!" I told the kids. "Let's go peek at Crazy Fabiano!"

He wasn't really crazy—he just didn't like to stay near the others. People said Crazy Fabiano was as old as Africa, that his spirit came from there and would go back when he died. He always sits on top of the Hill, looking far away, as far as Africa, maybe. We knew he wouldn't hurt us, but somehow it's fun to think he might. Kids would creep near and peek at him, then run away screaming.

So off we shot from where the houses hugged each other, toward the lonely place where only Crazy Fabiano lived. Even in the dark, my bare feet told me how to go. You must keep away from the edge of the Hill, otherwise, you'd go down forever into the black night water. Trying not to breathe, we crawled toward a smoking fire. Thorn bushes reached out scratchy hands to catch us, but we came to the place where Fabiano's feet had made the earth smooth in front of his door. His house, made all out of cans and bottles, winked like red and green and yellow eyes in the firelight.

Where was he? Was he sitting inside in the dark? Perhaps his eyes could see without light? If they saw all the way to Africa, they could! "He's not here, what a pity!" Louisa squeaked. But he was *somewhere*! Fear

81

spiders crawled over my neck and back. Something, someone was watching! Nilton felt it too. He turned—Fabiano was standing there, staring at *me*!

Like feathers blown out of your hand, the kids were gone! Fabiano's face showed in the firelight, black, wooden, with cracks for his African eyes. "Mama!" I cried, but Nilton put his hand on me to be quiet.

Pointing his cigar at me, Fabiano began to speak. "There, in Africa, I saw you. The sky spirits sent the birds, carrying bits of blue silk and bright, precious feathers to be a costume for your dance. The slow, long-legged birds that dance in the reeds and the small, quick birds that dance in the sky brought these. And when you began to dance, all in the village danced with you—men, women, the very old, and those about to be born. With great heat the people danced, till at last they became calm, and cool, and wise." Fabiano nodded and held up his cigar for me to say nothing. Then the bushes drank him up the way Pop swallows his little cup of black coffee.

We grabbed hands and ran and ran. But the words, the blue, silky, feathered words, ran with us so that when we fell down panting, safe near the houses and people, I asked, "Nilton, what was he saying? What did he mean?" But I really knew. *Oh, honey, you're chosen from all the others to be something high, to be the Queen!*

The kids came back, their eyes big. "I thought he was going to get you and take you to Africa," John from the Northeast said.

Louisa threw her arms around me. "Ooh, I'm so happy! I'm so happy you're all right, darling 'Tonia!

"Come on! Come on! Tell us! What did he do?! What did he say to you?!"

I looked at Nilton. "*You* tell them." Queens are too proud to say these things about themselves. Nilton scratched his head and began about the birds in Africa and how Fabiano said he saw me dancing there in a costume of blue silk and feathers.

"He's crazy, that Fabiano! I told you!"

"You never went to Africa, Maria Antonia. And besides—don't get mad—you're only a kid. Why would grown-ups follow you? They wouldn't!"

"They *will*," I wanted to say, but remembering the other time I boasted, I kept still. Everyone said again that he was crazy, that Fabiano. "Maybe he thinks he's the King of Africa!"

"Yeah—maybe he can jump off the cliff and fly there. Ha! Ha!"

For a while we just sat, tossing pebbles down the Hill and thinking, till the mothers began to call.

"Louisa!"

"Hambone! Get right home or I'll pepper your backside!"

One by one the kids got up and went away into the dark.

Nilton pretended he had a big old-fashioned hat on his head. He pulled it off and bowed to the ground. "I'll see you soon, Queen of Africa."

"You're crazy too." I gave him a push. But I couldn't stop the pleased smile from coming.

All the way home I was dancing in Africa, while tall birds swayed on their long legs and smaller ones picked with their beaks bright blue feathers for my dress.

12

Louisa and me were swinging in the hammock listening to her uncle's little radio. Roberto Antonio, the T.V. star, growled into Louisa's ear, "I'm a bad, bad wolf, but all the girls love me, Ooo-wowww!" Louisa is crazy about Roberto Antonio, as I've told you. I like him too, but not as much as Louisa; I have more serious things to think about. And Nilton is not very interested in singing stars. He was busy carving a wooden flute with his knife, a bit off here, a bit off there.

Today I was practically perfectly happy—hadn't Fabiano just about said I was going to be Queen? He must know things that other people don't.Still, maybe I should get him to put a spell on Teresinha so her hair would fall out. No, it's not necessary—I'd just forget "The Terrible Question" (who will the Director choose?) and think about fun and tricks like I used to, before "That Girl" came.

"Let's tell jokes, Louisa. I'll start. 'What is sour and green and sings?' "

Louisa said, "A singing pickle," because that's the right answer.

I shook my head, "Mr. Nascimento—he's sour and green and his nose is like a pickle!" It wasn't so funny, but we laughed till we shook right out of the hammock.

Louisa sat up. "Today you're like you used to be, 'Tonina.'"

Dona Elena was going by with her shopping bag. She always carried one stuffed with plastic bags and pieces of bread from the garbage cans in the City. Dona Elena never threw anything away; she stuffed it into a shopping bag. One of her flopping man's sneakers came off, and when she bent to tie it, she saw us. Smiling with no teeth, Dona Elena nodded and winked. She's always giving kids dumb presents—mostly dolls with missing arms or bald heads. The kids laugh at her and throw the dolls away right in front of her, but I don't. Somehow, she reminds me of Gramma. Of course, Gramma is neat and clean and not a bit crazy.

We watched her flip-flopping up the path. Her head was like a bird's nest with twigs of gray hair poking out

87

of the dirty, wrapped cloth. I wouldn't have been surprised to see birds peeking out. "Poor thing," I said, "she has nobody to be her husband or children."

"She's a loony, that's why!" Louisa snorted.

"Gramma's her friend, and she says Dona Elena wouldn't hurt a soul, even if she's crazy," I told Louisa.

There must be different kinds of crazy, like Fabiano— he's probably very smart and just doesn't want people to know it. But inside Dona Elena's head it's all a mess, like inside her shopping bag.

Climbing back into the hammock, I swung and wondered out loud, "What makes people crazy?"

Louisa said, "If their head got stepped on when they were a baby."

But Nilton thought, "When too many bad things happen to them, what can they do? They start to act crazy."

"Who wants to talk about crazy people?! I know the song that won First Prize at the Festival of Popular Music yesterday." Louisa began singing like a skinny bird, her voice scratching on the high parts.

"Ahhh! Ahhh!" What was that terrible crying coming from my house?! Louisa's mouth stayed open with no sound. My heart was knocking in me like it was trying to get out, as Nilton and I rushed toward the house.

Neighbors were so thick around my door I had to push them away to get to Mama. She was beating her hands in the air and making those awful cries. "What is it, Mama, what is it?!"

When she saw me, she began to weep. "The baby—
Little Sergio—he's gone!"

"He can't be gone! He must be here! Where is
Gramma?! She'll know." I grabbed our next-door neighbor. "Carolina, is it true?!" She nodded miserably.

Maybe he was under the chair cushion, the beds? I
rushed around, even lifting the pot lids. But there was
no little laughing baby. "Your Gramma went to Lindomar's for a package of laundry starch and your Mama
came to talk with me by the fence while the baby slept.
When she went in, the baby was gone, completely gone!"
Carolina wrung out a wet rag and put it to Mama's
forehead.

Everyone began to speak at once. "Pray to the Virgin!"
"Call the police!"

"What kind of thing is this?! Just because we live here,
it does not mean we are not citizens. This must be reported to the Police Chief, the Senators, the President
of the Republic!" Ernesto was shouting.

"Be calm, Elisabete, he is sure to be found. He didn't
walk away," somebody else said.

"Of course not! He is only fourteen months old, isn't
that right, Elisabete?" Mama nodded, sobbing again.
Friends and neighbors patted her and looked helpless.

"I'll run to get Pop! He'll find Little Sergio in a minute!" I raced out the door and raced in again. No one
could find Pop right now—his bus might be as far away
as the beach at Ipanema.

"The Gramma is here!" The crowd parted to let Gramma through.

"Oh, Gramma, Gramma, Little Sergio is missing! You know where he is, don't you?" Gramma looked at me, puzzled.

"What's this? Where is the baby?" She didn't know!

"He's been kidnapped! The scoundrels will not give him back till you pay a large sum of money." Ernesto had read a story like that in the paper about a Senator's son.

Mama screamed, "A large sum of money! Oh, dear God! Where would I get a large sum of money? Maria Antonia, run and tell your brothers and sisters."

"No need, child. You just rest here." Three neighbors ran to carry the news to the others of our family.

For the whole afternoon, Gramma, Mama, and me held on to each other, crying. Sometimes I ran to the bed and turned the covers over once again, as if Little Sergio might be there this time. By now the entire Hill of the Cashew Tree was in our house or waiting outside. My brothers and sisters arrived one by one with angry or tear-wet faces.

A policeman came up the Hill with a little pad of paper on which he wrote answers to his questions.

"The name of the lost person?"

"Little Sergio."

"No—the complete name."

"Sergio Antonio Luis dos Santos." (Such a long name

90

for such a little, little baby. My throat closed tight from the pain.)

"Where was he last seen?"

"Here, right here! Where else would he be?!"

"When was he last seen?"

"About 10:00, wouldn't you say?" Carolina looked at Mama.

"Let me see. It's 4:03 now." The policeman wrote that down. "Occupation?"

"Occupation? His occupation is 'baby'!"

Roberto was becoming very angry. "Why don't you do something?!"

"Now, now," the policeman tried to soothe him. "We will do everything possible to find him. I will make out a report and—oh, do you have a picture of the runaway person?"

"Runaway person! He is not a 'runaway'! And as for a picture, pictures are taken when you get married!" The policeman sighed and went away.

Pop burst in at the door. He had heard about Little Sergio as he started up our Hill. Everybody was talking about it. People were very sad for Mama and Pop. But I think they also liked the excitement of thinking, "Will that little child be found safe?" Mama fell on his chest and they wept together. "Who would want to hurt a little baby?" Mama kept saying.

It got dark outside. Our baby doesn't like to be in the dark!

Dona Elena was telling Mama, "No one would hurt him. Such an adorable baby. No, no." Carolina elbowed her aside to put fresh cloths on Mama's head and someone else tried to get Pop to drink some more coffee. My brothers were ready to run in the street and knock down the man who would do such a thing. And my sisters clung to one another and cried.

I sat with Nilton and knuckled away the tears hard.

"What can we do, Nilton?" He didn't answer. Instead he watched everything.

"Here is Dona Elena coming in the house for the fourth time. Does she come a lot to your house, Maria Antonia?"

"Sometimes she comes to see the baby and talk to Gramma. But why?"

"Come on!" Nilton pulled me out the door and yanked me down the steps.

"Where are we going? I can't leave Mama and Pop now!"

"We've got to get to Dona Elena's house before she does. We'll take my cart. Quick!" Nilton threw himself into the baby-buggy wagon. "Get in! Get in!" I did, too tired from the sadness to argue.

Nilton pushed off with me holding tight around his middle. Down we shot, the buggy wheels each going a different way and the hard bounces spanking our bottoms. Down, down till my teeth rattled like marbles. "Stop, you cra-zy Nil-ton!" the words jiggled out.

"She has the baby!" Nilton shouted over his shoulder.

Of course! Dona Elena had our baby! "Go faster, Nilton!" I screamed.

We were almost at the bottom. Nilton whirled the steering wheel so that we screeched around, running a little way up again, and stopping in front of Dona Elena's. Nilton threw himself at the door. The rusty latch broke

right off so that he fell inside. It was like a garbage pile—
broken chairs, empty shampoo bottles, bent and leaning
pots. More than anything, there were dolls: crippled, one-
eyed, rag-dressed dolls, dolls, dolls.

Only one doll was not broken—Little Sergio! He was
nested in rags and old pillows with a bashed rubber toy
swinging over him on a string. His face shone over the
rag covers like a happy little sun when he saw me. He
didn't know he was kidnapped!

I knelt and squeezed him to me. "Oh, baby, little baby."
Rocking him, I kissed the soft, sweet top of his head.
"Don't cry. Sister's got you."

"Maria Antonia! Come on! We've got to get him out
of here!"

As I got up we saw that Little Sergio had on a new
blue playsuit with a pink elephant on the front. Nilton
looked at me. Then he grabbed my arm and pushed me
toward the door. "Is Crazy Elena coming right now?!"
Little needles of fear pricked me, but we didn't see her.

By the rocky, back ways we hurried, Nilton pulling
the wagon and me holding tight to the baby. Our hands
and knees got skinned and bloody, we hurried so fast.
But we didn't care. Little Sergio was safe!

When the silent crowd in front of my house saw us,
they began to shout. People hugged Nilton, the baby,
and me, and yelled for Mama to come out.

"Elisabete, your baby is here!" Mama rushed to the
steps, her eyes wildly looking. When I put Little Sergio

in her arms, a great cheer went up and people began to cry. Pop, Gramma, the brothers and sisters all had to kiss the baby, hug Nilton and me, and thank the Lord.

Then I saw him on the side, a man in a whole suit of gray soft cloth, with a smooth-shaped hat on his head. Smiling a little, he took out a pad of paper. With a wave of his ringed fingers, he began to write. "It's the reporter from the *Jornal do Brasil*," people were telling each other.

"What is the name of the little girl who rescued the baby?" A hundred voices began to explain at once who I was. "But who had kidnapped the infant?" The voices were silent. I sneaked a look at Nilton. We each knew what the other was thinking—"Don't tell this man about Dona Elena. They'll take her to jail."

"We found him, Nilton and me," I began. "He was in a little bed by the rocks down there. And he was all right."

"But, my child, who had taken him?"

"We don't know. . . ." The man looked annoyed. Then he had a new idea. "Tell me, little girl, what do you like to do in school?"

I looked at the ground and twisted my curl. Finally, I said, "Sometimes I go to school, but mostly I dance."

"Ah, yes, of course. You belong to the Samba dancers here on The Hill of the Cashew Tree."

I stopped twisting the curl and scraping my toe along the ground. "I'm going to carry the flag for The Cashew Tree in the procession at Carnival when I'm grown."

"Oh, ho," he laughed. "I suppose every little girl around

96

here thinks that." He patted my head. I was going to shout at him, "I'm not every little girl, you stupid!" I caught myself, but it was too late. Boasting, that's what I was doing. Boasting about the secret! That could bring very bad luck. But somehow, I really *wanted* it to be in the paper. If it's in the paper, it's going to be true!

The reporter went away and Pop and Mama thanked all the neighbors. They shut the door. Only our own family was there, and Nilton, of course. "Maria Antonia, you didn't tell what really happened."

I nodded. "You see, Nilton saw Dona Elena coming here too many times. So he rode me fast down to her house and we found the baby there."

"But why didn't you say it was Dona Elena?" everyone wanted to know.

I looked at Gramma. "Nilton and me were afraid they'd take Dona Elena to jail. And she did try to take good care of him."

"You stupid!" Carlos shouted. "She'll do it again!"

"No," Pop said. "We can tell everyone to look out for their little ones. And we'll talk to her. Gramma will tell her she must never do it again."

Everyone looked at Mama. She said nothing for a while. "I think she won't do it again." Then she hugged Nilton and me. "You kids are smarter than the police."

Then, after everybody kissed the baby good night at least five times and saw him safe in bed by Gramma's side, they too fell asleep. Except me—I chewed the cor-

97

ner of my nightie. Maybe I shouldn't have told the man from the newspapers? *Oh, yes, honey, you're going to be the Queen, so why not let them all know?*

Half-awake, half-dreaming, I saw a gorgeous Maria Antonia floating out of the newspaper and dancing over the whole City.

Before anyone was awake, I put on my good dress and sat on the steps to wait. The skirt was too short to cover my knees because I've had it for four years. But it was still pretty. The tiny flowers showed like white sprinkled stars in the morning. And there were new red ribbons to tie up each sleeve. Nervously I tied them and untied them and pulled the skirt down over my legs.

The kids started coming in front of my house. They were waiting too for the first person to come up the path from the City. It was Jercino, the garbage man, coming from his job. Under his arm was the newspaper, and the kids buzzed around him like mosquitoes, begging for a look at it. (I stayed calm on the top step.) "Here, you can have it," he told them. "I read the sports already on the bus."

Everybody was snatching, but John from the Northeast got it and put the paper in Nilton's hands. Only Nilton could read well enough for this. He sat on the bottom step and, touching his finger to his tongue, began to turn the big, crackly sheets. I couldn't help leaning forward a little.

Where was it? On the front there was a picture of a lady with her hair in a shiny black roll on her head. She was looking over her shoulder and smiling backward with dark lipstick.

" 'Society Lady Visits Orphans,' " Nilton read.

"No, that's not the one." Sebastian couldn't wait.

"He knows that!" the others shouted. Nilton's fingers walked up and down the second page, the third, the fourth, and the paper was almost finished. His finger stopped at the bottom of the last page.

" 'Shantytown Infant Found,' " he read. "That's it!" "That's it!" Everybody was pushing each other in the ribs and grinning. " 'The sister and friend of a fourteen-month-old inhabitant of The Hill of the Cashew Tree found and returned to its mother the baby, Sergio Antonio Luis dos Santos. . . .' "

100

"The sister! That's you, Maria Antonia!" Louisa screamed.

Nilton went on, " 'It could not be determined who had kidnapped the child, but the sister reported finding "Little Sergio" safe among the rocks near their home, six hours after the child was reported missing. Police were preparing to order a helicopter search when Maria Antonia Carmen dos Santos, and her companion, Nilton Rodriguez, appeared with the infant and placed it in the frantic mother's arms. The brave little girl, who is a dancer for The Cashew Tree, told the reporter that it is her ambition to be Flag Bearer when she is grown. The entire Hill, which had been preparing for Carnival, returned again to its rehearsals and costume making after the tragedy turned to happiness.' "

Right there, for the whole world to see—"It is her ambition to be Flag Bearer for The Cashew Tree when she is grown!" The kids all gazed at me like I really was something. I smiled softly, kindly down at them.

People began coming to congratulate Mama on the baby's safe return and to hear about Dona Elena. Almost everyone thought it was not right to send her to jail. "We must be kinder to her, invite her sometimes to come and take supper with our families," Dona Flora suggested. But somebody else said Dona Elena was too smelly.

"Maybe," I said, "if Dona Elena had a big doll to dress and hold, she could think it was her baby."

"It isn't the same, child," everybody laughed.

"Yes, but after all, she is . . ." Dona Laura made a circle with her finger to her head, ". . . and it just might work."

Dona Laura is very bossy—if she says a thing, the others do it. It was decided that Carolina would buy a baby doll with blond curls and a pink bonnet and dress when she went to the Saturday market. (If it was not too expensive.)

The ladies again started praising me and Nilton. "These young ones have such courage and ambition! You'll see Maria Antonia at the front of the Procession when she's as big as her sisters." It was like a sweetness in my mouth. I am the one who's going to be chosen!

All afternoon I sat on the step, looking at the black-and-white marks on the paper that told about me. It seemed as though it were already true what it said. Then John from the Northeast swore, "_____! Enough with this old newspaper! Let's do something!" I smiled like someone dreaming and shook my head.

They all left to go to Auntie Serafina and Uncle Waldemar's. We kids like to wriggle under the porch with the chickens and wait for Auntie and Uncle to come out. Auntie and Uncle would sit in their chairs for hours, rocking and watching the City and the sea like a raggedy King and Queen.

We'd wait till we heard the rockers *screek, screek.* Then we'd wait for Auntie's stomach to go *urrgle, urrgle,* and for Uncle's to answer, *ruggle, ruggle*. That always made us fall down in the sneezy dust, laughing so hard! The chickens would glare and tell each other, "They're crazy." Of course, we couldn't hurt Auntie and Uncle's feelings—they were as deaf as two onions. But now, that all seemed so childish for someone as important as me.

When the kids came back, I said, "Louisa, get me a cup of water, will you?"

She gave me a funny look. "Are you sick or something?"

"No, I'm just thirsty." Louisa went inside and came back with a tin cup of water from the brown pottery jar. I sipped, smiling slightly, the way important people drink.

Nilton and Hambone were dancing around, kicking the soccer ball to each other. John from the Northeast and the others joined them. Soon the game got hot. "Hey, you touched it with your finger!" John shouted at Hambone.

"Never! You're crazy!" They pushed their faces close together, their hands on their hips, and their eyebrows made angry Ws.

Now, I'm not very interested in soccer, but I felt a person like me should decide who was right. Bending down from the top step, I waved my hand—"Hambone *did* touch it with his finger."

"Go stick beans up your nose! Just because you're in the newspaper, you think you're so special!"

"No, but . . ."

103

Here, everyone began shouting. "He did!" "I saw it perfectly, he didn't!" "He did!"

When I tried to speak again, Gabriel shouted, "Shut up, you old, wrinkled monkey!"

"Do you know who you are talking to?!" I was going to punch him, but the others began, "He's right! You're too bossy!"

"And snooty! She thinks she's better than anybody else!"

"You can't tell everybody what to do—'Get me a cup of water, I'm the Queen. Oh, my . . .' " Hambone wriggled his hips, pretending he was me. And everyone laughed.

I was so mad! Clenching my fists, I was going to fight them all. But they just walked away, even Louisa. Hambone called back, "Bossy! You're so full of yourself!" Nilton didn't bother to look back.

I yelled, "It's not my fault! I can't help it if I'm the one!" But they were gone.

"It's time!" Nilton's head poked in the window.

"The rehearsal is beginning!" Mama cried. "Where's the baby?!" Grabbing him, she ran to the door.

Maria Clara shrieked, "Where are my slippers?"

"Here," Carlos said. "If your boyfriend knew what a pain you are, he'd marry Angelina like he was going to." Maria Clara threw a slipper at him.

Everybody was rushing out of their houses, laughing and calling to one another. They couldn't stop smiling— except me. I sneaked a look at Nilton. He seemed to have forgotten this afternoon.

Boom-da! Boom-da! "The band, it's starting, Nilton!" Everybody was tumbling down the Hill onto the white pavement, like coffee beans dumped out of the sack.

"Over here!" Louisa screamed, waving from where our gang was, by the band. Little two- and three-year-olds were there dancing too. They learn Samba when they're learning to talk. They're so cute; I love to play with them. But tonight the fear was squeezing me—what if I didn't get chosen? *Now, honey, didn't the newspaper say it?*

The kids couldn't wait for the grown-ups. Hambone did trick steps, looking cool, like he didn't know how fast his feet were going. The big girls danced as if they didn't care at all. Then they looked quickly to see which boys were watching. Louisa threw her arm around me. She forgets everything, so I guess she forgot about this afternoon too.

"Dance, dance Samba, dance Samba!" the drums talked inside my chest. "Dance, dance Samba!" groaned the quicas—it sounds like a fat man out of breath when they pull the strings inside the tin cans. And the rattles were always whispering, "You must dance Samba, you must dance Samba."

The Director's whistle shrieked, ordering the band to "Start!" "Stop!" and "Begin again!" Directors and Presidents ran about, giving orders and waving their arms. Such excitement and happiness—except for me. I chewed the end of my ponytail.

106

Teresinha's sandals beat the pavement fast as rain. Teresinha was wriggling and shaking—every part of her was dancing! And all that hair! She was throwing it around like she was so proud of it. "Oh, she's good tonight." Louisa wagged her head. "But you're better." She hugged me.

"Silence, please!" Our President, Mr. Hector da Silva, came on the bandstand. He was going to make a speech. Everybody said, "Shhh! Shhh!" to everybody else, so it took a few minutes till the last baby became quiet.

For a while, Mr. da Silva gazed seriously over our heads. Then he began to speak. "As you know, our theme for the Procession is 'Salute to the Soul of Brazil'! This soul once found its expression in the Lords and Ladies of the Emperor Dom Pedro's court. But today, Ladies and Gentlemen, it finds its expression in the Samba dancers of The Hill of the Cashew Tree!" Cheers shook the air. He got louder. "And so we must rehearse tonight and dance on that wonderful night—only forty-eight hours from now—so as to show our great city, Rio, that *we* are the champions!!" The crowd cheered and beat on their instruments till finally they had to stop. Mr. da Silva wiped his eyes—he always gets tears in his eyes when he talks about The Cashew Tree and Samba.

Louisa fell on top of me giggling. "His eyes are like two fried eggs." They did look just like that, but instead of laughing, I scolded her. "Louisa, you nut, you can't laugh at the President!"

She giggled more—her giggling fits can last a long time, but Hambone warned, "He's coming! Feijaozinbo!" We jumped to our places.

The Director of the Children's Group came dashing up. His nickname is "Little Beans," but we're not supposed to call him that. "Little ones! Little ones! Not like that!" Frowning, he pulled me and Teresinha to the front line.

"That's so he can decide who's better," John of the Northeast hissed in my ear. I knew that!

I looked all around so as not to look at Teresinha. On the side, Gramma sat with Little Sergio. She was holding him round the stomach, dancing him to the music, and he was pushing with his toes on her lap. So cute! I had to go see him. Holding his little hands and clapping them, I whispered,"You'll see, Little Sergio. It's going to be me out front. And when you're a big boy, you'll say, 'That's my sister, Maria Antonia, the Queen of the Samba!' "

Gramma's friend Aurelia came to see her. "Give me the baby and you dance for a little."

Of course, Gramma can't jump and move herself all over like we do. She does mostly rocking and smiling and patting one hand on the other. But she keeps making Samba.

"Dance, Gramma, dance!" I cheered her.

The Director's whistle was screaming, "To your places! Right now! Begin! Go!" and we did—*Pow!* Like little devils, that's how our group dances! Naturally, each one has their own way. Louisa dances all around, laughing and talking to everyone. John and Hambone are jumping clowns, spinning their tambourines on one finger and grinning.

For me, it's different. When I'm really dancing, I don't see anyone; I don't talk to anyone. It's very serious. But it's happiness. I don't know how to say it! Maybe it's serious happiness. Anyway, *tonight* I couldn't stop watching Teresinha. Her feet—were they faster than mine?! Her smile—didn't it say, "I'm the best"? But everyone will see that it is *me* who is best!

Harder and harder we practiced, till one o'clock, two o'clock. People's sweaty faces were polished shiny in the lights as they swallowed cold bottles of beer and soda, their heads way back. Nilton lay flat on the concrete, gazing up. We like to do that, Nilton and me. We look past all the mixed-up legs and bodies and faces, past the white lights to the black square where the stars are dancing. But tonight I couldn't. Worry was chewing my bones.

Gramma waved for me to come. Little Sergio was sleeping in one arm. The other she made into a circle for me. I shook my head. "My goodness," Louisa said. "How quiet you are, Maria Antonia! But you'll see, you're dancing so good tonight, like a little wildcat. Feijaozinbo's going to choose you." I tried to smile and say, "No, no." You have to act as though you aren't very good, even if you are. For luck, it was important to do that.

Teresinha flipped by, her skirt swinging. My own skirt— it was too stingy to really swirl! Why didn't I see that before?! Louisa poked me. "The Director is looking at you!" Down in the elevator went my stomach. Feijaozinbo *was* staring at me. He took his handkerchief and slowly patted the sweat off all over his face. Then he looked where Teresinha was chattering with her friends. All the kids were watching. They saw him raise his hand and—scratch his eyebrow!

"Little girl, come here." Feijaozinbo curled his finger. I started toward him. "No." He shook his head and pointed. "You." Teresinha flounced her skirt right up to him. He began to explain about the part, the special part in front where everyone would see her, like a little Queen!

The kids looked out of the sides of their eyes at me. Nilton said, "Maybe she's not so good—she just looks good." I turned my head in case any tears were coming.

Louisa put her face close and "sissed" like a mad cat. "I think you should fight her, Maria Antonia. I'd smack her face and pull her hair out. Who does she think she is, coming here and taking your place!"

"All these lights are giving me a headache." I pushed past Louisa, past the people on the hot, bright pavement, past the lights. The dark was cool and I was hot from the shame. Clenching my fists, I ran up the path. I would pull Teresinha's long hair all out! I'd tear her skirt in little pieces so she couldn't go to the Procession! If only I didn't say to the kids that it would be me! *Honey, it's supposed to be you. It must be a mistake.* Yes, it's just a mistake!

I'd come as far as Auntie Serafina's. From here you could see all the lights in the far apartments and the winking, shining ocean. Everything was winking and shining because of the water in my eyes. Lucky that Auntie Serafina wasn't sitting on her porch now. She'd say, "Why, child, you're crying."

The moonlight made the ocean into a silver cloth with black sequins on it. But what did I care now? Sylvia was sleeping in Hungry Joe's mango tree. "Yahhh!" I shook the tree till her feathers flew and her eyes went around in her head. "You dumb chicken!" I yelled. Sylvia was still clucking "Bad girl" when I came to my house. Banging open the door, I fell on Gramma's bed and pushed my face into Gramma's quilt. "Ah-boo-boo!" For a long while I cried. "It should have been me! I was born lucky and I'm supposed to be happy! Ah-boo-boo!"

Then it stopped, the sound like a giant heart beating. Voices were coming up the path. Snuffling my wet nose on the quilt, I pretended I was asleep. Mama was saying, "She must be here. Why does she worry us like that?" Poppa's voice—"What a disappointment for the child. Tonight she wasn't at her best. I think she was looking at the other one, Teresinha, and missed her steps."

111

Snap! The light bulb winked on and the family was coming into the house. "Shh, she's here, asleep," Gramma said. I squeezed my eyes tighter. Gramma put the baby next to me and she went to sleep with Regina.

The light bulb's burning eye winked closed. Snores and sighs and sleeping sounds. Quiet tears sneaked out of my eyes.

Someone this sad couldn't possibly sleep. But, then, I was sleeping too.

In the morning, I didn't speak to anyone. "Come on, your life isn't over." Roberto smiled at me. And Maria Clara said, "You'll have other chances." My life was ruined! It could never be good again! They just didn't understand!

Even the baby couldn't make me smile. Mama said, "You're being silly. 'One loses, another gains.' That's what life is. Come, I'll fix your hair so it's long and pretty." She sat me on a chair and took the jar of Alberto's pink hair oil, Creme Longo.

"Hey!" He started to say something, but Mama winked.

"Let her use some." Taking a pink-smelling glob from

the jar, she stroked it on my head, combing and pulling the hairs to make them straighter.

"Ouch!" I yelled.

"That doesn't hurt." Mama busily pulled it some more.

The Creme Longo didn't help.It's still just a little bunch of crinkly hairs! A tear came sliding down my nose. Ducking away from Mama, I ran to where Gramma was sewing in the corner. More tears and more, like the rains in the winter that slide the houses and people away. I couldn't stop them. "Ah-boo-boo!" Gramma patted me. "I know, I know, my dear little girl."

"It should have been me, because, because—I wanted it more!" I bellowed.

Mama said, "What a spoiled girl!"

"You're a spoiled girl!" I yelled at Mama, but she didn't smack me. After a while, the hard tears stopped and it just ached inside.

Louisa was calling from outside, "Maria Antonia!"

Slowly I went to the door. "What do you want?"

Louisa sat down on the steps. "Maria Antonia, you should fight her. She stole that part from you, and if you punched her face all up and ripped her dress, she couldn't go in the Procession. You should beat her up like Angelina beat up Maria Laura when Maria Laura stole her boyfriend." I didn't see that fight, but Louisa saw them all.

"What a fight!" Louisa went on. "Angelina told her, 'You think you can steal anybody's boyfriend you want—

114

well, you can't!' And she smacked her in the mouth. Then Maria Laura kicked Angelina in the shins. And they were screaming, 'He loves *me* better!' "

"Who won the fight?"

"Angelina did—you should have seen what she did to Maria Laura."

"And did she get her boyfriend back?"

"No, because he already liked Gloria."

A movie was going in my head—of me telling Teresinha, "You think you are a hot potato! You think you are better than anybody else, coming around here with all that long hair! And your skirt with so much material! Why do you always smile like you know you're so pretty? Well, I can dance better than you—I was born to dance Samba!" Angry tears stung my eyes.

Louisa was watching me. "Ha! Don't be afraid of her. She can't fight. I'll arrange everything for you." She jumped up. "You can't let Teresinha take what's yours. I'll tell her you want to fight her, okay?!" Louisa's skinny legs were already carrying her away. Her little pigtail stood straight out from excitement.

"Tell her I'll fix her! Tell her she's an ugly rat!"

"Yeah!" Louisa yelled back. "In half an hour! By the kite-flying place!" I sat down again on the step and twisted that poor little curl of hair. "Don't do that," Mama always says. "How do you expect to get your hair straight?"

"Hey, Maria Antonia! You're going to fight Teresinha!" John of the Northeast and Hambone came running up. Louisa had passed them on her way to Teresinha. Soon the whole Children's Group was here to see Maria Antonia, "The Fighter."

"Oh, boy! This is going to be some fight, eh, Maria Antonia?" Sebastian winked and rubbed his hands as if the fight was a chicken pie and he could eat it.

"Let's get away from here. My mother doesn't like fights," I told them.We moved toward the fight place with everybody showing me how to do it. *Bam! Oof!* They ducked their heads and punched; they circled like bees.

Nilton came riding up in his wagon. *Racketty, rack-etty*, it complained and everything seemed about to come off, but it didn't. He came next to me. "You want to fight Teresinha?"

"She's taking my place! Everybody says it should be me. (Really, only Louisa said that.) Anyway, it's probably just a mistake."

Nilton leaned forward and fixed the rubber sandal he used for the brake on his wagon. "You think too much about beating Teresinha. You're beginning to look like Damon, 'The Worrier.' Even if you win, that doesn't mean the Director will give you the place."

"I don't care—she's so stuck-up! I'm gonna show her!" Nilton shrugged and got up to go. He jumped in his wagon and pushed with his foot onto the path that goes down to Zeca's.

"Aren't you coming to my fight?"

"Nope," and he was gone. I could hear the pebbles

116

skittering and the people jumping to get out of Nilton's way. "Look out, boy! You'll end up in the hospital!" "Or he'll put somebody else there!"

Arnaldo was coming up the path. "Oh, what do you want, you pest?!" He hadn't even asked for anything yet.

"Have you got something for me?"

"No, I haven't! You stupid, you'll take anything! But I'm not like you!" I was shouting. "I'm the best or nothing!" Arnaldo backed away, looking scared.

"Heyyy!" Louisa was waving. There was no time to be sorry about Arnaldo. I hurried to where the army of kids was waiting for me. On this highest part of the Hill, the wind was nosing at the kites, but the boys had thrown them down. It was my fight they wanted to see. Louisa came hurrying, very important, and took my arm. "She's right over there with her brother!"

Maybe this was the first time I really looked at her. She didn't look so stuck-up. She had on a dress like mine, the flowers washed off from so many times under the pump. You know what Teresinha reminds me of?! The little, fluffy dog with a pink bow Dona Laura has that everybody pets. It shakes if it thinks anybody's mad at it. I told Louisa, "If she hadn't done what she did to me, I wouldn't have to beat her up."

"Of course," Louisa said, pulling my arm.

"Come on." Hambone and John of the Northeast patted my back. "You're gonna be the winner. Give her a smack on the snoot, Maria Antonia!"

117

"Fava beans! Seven for a penny!" John's cousin was selling salted beans to anybody who had a penny.

"Insult her, Maria Antonia! This fight is never going to get started," Sebastian grumbled.

"Hey!" Hambone warned. "Mauro's coming."

Teresinha's brother was moving toward us, trying to act like Big Stuff. "What's the matter, Skinny-Legs, your girl doesn't want to fight?"

Mauro never should have called Louisa that. She shouted, "Maria Antonia does *so* want to fight!" And she cracked her knuckles hard on top of Mauro's head so that tears came out of his eyes. Mauro kicked Louisa's skinny shins. "Awoww!" A screaming noise came out of Louisa like a fire engine. Then she played the rhythms on Mauro's head. Teresinha was weeping like a scared little kid. I walked over.

"Why are you crying? I didn't even hit you yet," I said, taking the hanky from my pocket and putting it in Teresinha's hand. Disgusted with myself, I turned away. The Queen of the Samba doesn't fight to be Queen. She just *is*.

Back there, they were all fighting Mauro and Louisa's fight over again. But I went slowly home. Peeking over the windowsill, I could see Mama pouring water from the carrying tin into the cool brown pottery jar in the corner. There was a picture on the tin of a happy lady with a big, strong chest. She had a giant basket full of olives on her head, and her mouth was open, with singing coming out.

That lady never got tired of carrying her basket, but Mama did, bringing the full tins of water all the way from the pump at the bottom of the Hill. And this time

Mama had to do it without me. She set the tin down and made her "where is that child?" face. I hoped Mama didn't know about the fight—she gets very mad if her daughters go near one. "Girls who fight give husbands a fright," she says. But that's not true. Everybody I know who's married has fights—before they're married, and after.

"Mama," I said loudly, "I'm here to help you." I thought she'd say, "It's too late for that now." Instead she put her finger to her lips.

"Gramma's lying down." My Gramma is always busy, wiping up where Sergio spills, cleaning vegetables, stealing a piece from the tail of a shirt to cover a hole in the top. I wasn't used to seeing her in the bed, like a little Gramma doll.

"What's the matter, Gramma?" I hurried to her.

"Nothing, nothing," she smiled. "I felt like taking a small rest, to be ready for Carnival, you know."

"Oh, yes, Gramma. It's good for you to rest!" Pushing away the fear about Gramma to its secret hiding place, I told her, "Mama and me will get supper ready."

I began rubbing the forks and setting them out on the table by each of the places. Mama didn't seem to know about the fight—I looked sideways at her now and then. She was just holding Little Sergio on her hip and stirring the stew with her big wooden spoon. That was good luck!

The darkness outside makes the light bulb brighter. And the magazine people come smiling out of the walls.

121

When my part of the supper work is done, I like to look at them and wonder, "Why have these kids always got new clothes? And how can they keep those white shoes and socks so perfectly white?" For a while I was forgetting. Then the picture came back—the Director was pointing at Teresinha and the shame made me hot again.

That's why I didn't go to meet Pop, though it's always me who's the first to see him. *Bam!* The door crashed open and Carlos rushed in, tossing his soccer ball under the bed. "Are you still being a baby?"

"Go stick beans in your ears," I told him. Then Pop came, with a special smile for me, and Roberto, Alberto, and Regina, followed by Maria Helena and Maria Clara.

In a minute the house was bubbling like the stew, the brothers and sisters joking and telling what happened at their jobs and on the street. When they asked me, "What have you been doing today?" I knew they hadn't heard about the fight. "Stop trying to make me feel better," I snapped.

Gramma waved to me from her bed when all of us were seated at the table. Everybody began talking about how gorgeous this one's costume was and how jealous another was about it. Regina smiled more than ever, dreaming over her supper. She said, "Tomorrow night is going to be the best night of my life." I could tell she was thinking how her dress fitted on her so sweetly and how beautiful her dark hair and tan skin would look in front of all the people on the Avenue.

"Every time, it's the best time," Gramma said softly from the bed.

"Yes, yes," the whole family agreed, except one—

"It's not going to be the best night of my life," I announced.

"Why not, my little girl?" Pop asked.

"Because," I suddenly decided, "I'm not going to be there. I'm not going in the Procession."

Everybody stopped eating. "That's nonsense," Mama said.

"Our Hill needs you," Alberto tried to tell me. "Hah!" is what I thought of that.

"She's just trying to get attention!" Carlos almost choked on a big mouthful.

Pop said, "You're a fine little dancer. We do need you."

"They won't even see that I'm not there."

"If you don't do your part," Maria Clara said, "next year your Director might not let you go in the Procession, even if you want to." I wouldn't listen to any of them—they couldn't understand how it feels for a Queen to be "just one of the dancers," one of "the kids."

"I don't know what has got into that child!" Mama said. "She'll change her mind when she sees everybody getting ready to go." She began to eat again.

The rest did too. Roberto began biting off a piece of bread as if he were mad at it. "Did you hear that Portela's story has parts just like ours?! They've stolen that exact scene where the Emperor salutes the people for their bravery."

"Well," Pop answered, "you can't exactly say they stole it. After all, everybody knows about that. It's Brazilian history. Please pass the bread."

On and on they jabbered, only about Carnival and the Procession. How boring it was! I got up and went to Gramma's bed. She was sleeping. Her supper had just a little nibbled from it and I took it to Mama. "It's good she's asleep," Mama said, and she and the sisters quietly dipped the plates in the pan of soapy, then the pan of clear water.

I went and sat on the step, twisting and untwisting that curl. People were going back and forth, laughing and complimenting each other on their costumes. "Dona Margarete, you are a sight to delight!" "Ah, the Senhor is truly magnificent himself."

"Hey, Maria Antonia." Nilton was sitting beside me before I even saw him coming. He didn't ask about the fight, but I was sure he knew. Instead, he put the cage of little brown birds on my lap.

"You didn't sell them!" I was glad for that. "What will you do with them?"

"Oh, I don't know yet. . . ." Nilton took out his knife and began to smooth the little roof with its tiny carvings on each corner. "Maybe I'll keep them, maybe I'll give them to somebody." He whittled some more.

124

"Nilton, did you know I'm not going in the Procession?" (How could he know? I hadn't decided that till an hour ago.) But I wanted to hear what he'd say.

"Stop acting silly. Look, for you I've decided to let the birds go." He knew I hated the little things to be caught in the cage. "Watch!" Nilton opened the matchstick door. The little birds stayed in the corner—maybe they didn't believe they could go? Then, like shooting stars, they were gone into the sky.

Watching, I felt like I was flying too. Still, I said, "That won't help—I'm not going in the Procession."

"You can't do that to The Cashew Tree, Maria Antonia. Nobody does that."

"I can do what I like," putting my chin up proudly.

"Then you are a big baby." Nilton turned away, disgusted. He took his cage and was gone as quickly as he'd come. I wanted to call after him, "But all the signs said it would be me! This is just a mistake, a big mistake!" Instead, I sat there, smoothing my dress over my knees and rubbing away the wet spots that kept coming down on it.

"Maria Antonia! Maria Antonia! I have something awful to tell you! But maybe I better not, you'll be so mad. And you won't believe it! I didn't either but I saw it myself. He really did take her to the movies last night!" Louisa was almost pulling out her pigtail she was so excited.

"What are you talking about?" But I already knew. It was like a bad dream that you have—and then it happens! Nilton wasn't my boyfriend anymore. He took Teresinha to the movies.

"What do I care?" I tried to say that as though I really didn't, but my voice came out too high.

"Maybe he'll come back? She's nothing. Everybody thinks she's pretty with that little nose, but I don't. Anyway, you're a million times better a dancer than she is! Why did he leave you, Maria Antonia?"

"How should I know? And I told you it was nothing to me." But my mind was jumping around; to yesterday and Nilton saying, "You are a big baby"; to all the times I was mean and bossy. You can't keep a boyfriend if you always pick on him. *Honey, you don't need a boyfriend. You're going to be so famous you won't need anybody.* Yes, yes, that's true!

"Who are you talking to, Maria Antonia? There's nobody here." Louisa went on jabbering. You don't have to answer her. She talks anyway.

Was I madder or sadder? If it was sadder, I'd put that away till I was by myself. It's easier to be madder. And oh, yes, I could get real mad at what we saw now! Behind Lindomar's something very bad was going on. Big, tough guys from another hill were teasing Arnaldo. One wore a sweat shirt that said, "I'm a Bottle Baby." Right on his fat stomach there was a picture of a beer bottle with a rubber nipple on it. "What a stupid," I thought. Another had eyes like little stones. He wouldn't let Arnaldo go past.

"Stop that!" I rushed up to "Bottle Baby" and kicked him like a judo fighter. "Hai! Eeee!" He just caught my foot and held it.

"Look at this—she likes the dummy."

127

With your foot in the air you can't do a thing. Louisa screamed, "I'm coming to help you!" But "Stone Eyes" grabbed her by her little pigtail. There we were, Louisa and me, puppies, held up by the backs of our necks!

Those rotten guys laughed and laughed. One of them told Arnaldo, "Donkey, nice donkey, bend over so I can ride you." Poor Arnaldo. He tried to be a good donkey, but things began to fall out of his pockets. My gold button, a rubber mouse with no tail, smoothed-out candy papers he was saving, Popsicle sticks.

"Ai! Ai!" Arnaldo cried and reached for his toys. But that boy kept riding and kicking him with his heels. Fire burned in me, but I pretended to cry. "Let me go! *Please* let me go! I won't do anything, I promise." "Bottle Baby" dropped my foot.

"She knows who's the boss."

"You big stupid!" Like a firecracker I exploded. No! A string of firecrackers that go off one after the other. Punching, kicking, yelling, and butting my head into "Stone Eyes' " stomach. He let go of Louisa fast! There was plenty of biting and scratching then, I can tell you.

Whether we could have beaten them all, I don't know. Because Lindomar and her husband came running out of the back of her store. Each one of her hands was as big around as the loaf of bread for a whole family. She swung them and used her feet like Pelé. And those awful boys were the soccer ball. Her little husband cheered

128

her, and when the beer bottle shirt ran away, he shouted, "Goal!"

Lindomar was sweating and smiling at us. "Men, watch out when women get angry. Eh, girls?" She took Arnaldo's arm and led him into her store. There she stuffed his pockets with cookies, and she gave him a broken funnel that pleased him even more.

Louisa and I started home. "Wow! What a swell fight, Maria Antonia! You were terrific!"

"You were too. But don't tell anybody. My mother will be mad if she finds out." Louisa ran off to tell everybody I was sure. But what could I do?

I went along kicking little puffs of dirt. Is it really true? Is Louisa just making that up. But I knew she wasn't. How could it happen? *She's prettier. And that's how men and boys are. You can't trust them.* No, I mean she *is* prettier, but it could be something else. I've been so worried about getting the part. After all, to be Queen you have to think only of that. *Naturally.* But maybe I sort of *acted* like I was better than the other kids, a *little bit* snooty? *But those others can't dance like you; they're just not as important as you, that's all. What's the harm if you're only saying what is true?* But if you're too snooty, nobody likes you. *So what? What do they know? What do you care?*

My eyes were on the dirt, so I didn't see him come. He was there, like a magician, in front of me, Nil-

129

ton. "Hello, Maria Antonia." What could I say to him?! What should I do?! "I heard about your fight, yours and Louisa's. It's good you helped Arnaldo."

I nodded. Then I just said it—"Why did you take Teresinha to the movies?"

Nilton thought for a minute. He looked sort of sad. Then he said, "I guess I just wanted to be with somebody who isn't worried all the time about being famous."

"I can't help it! I have to be that way! Why don't you say the truth—she's prettier than me!"

Nilton looked at me, long and quiet. I had to turn away my eyes. When I looked again, he was gone.

Mama was waiting for me with the flyswatter in her hand—she has two, one for flies. "What did I tell you about girls fighting?" If I told her the fight was on account of Arnaldo, she probably wouldn't even spank me. She didn't spank hard anyway, just little swats. It's embarrassing, that's all.

I pulled my dress up in the back and bent over. I almost wished she would hurt. Then I wouldn't feel the other pain so much—Nilton is gone. He was the nicest boyfriend! And I'll never get another one!

Because it was here, The Night on the Avenue, there was no peace for me anywhere. In my house, in everybody's house, there was such excitement, such shrieks of happiness, such running next door to be pinned or have a ruffle sewn on. Dona Flor, who had a sewing machine, didn't get up from it for two days and nights. "Please, Dona Flor, you're so kind—just this fold, see— here it doesn't fall quite right."

Gramma had helped everybody to get their costumes ready. My sisters, shepherdesses of the Emperor's Court, had very short, pink satin skirts, loaded with green se-

131

quins. Pink-and-green feathers waved on their heads. One hundred times they had stood in front of Gramma and the mirror, swinging their skirts to be sure they looked perfect.

Sergio and me stayed on Gramma's bed. Sergio sucked Gramma's finger and I patted her hand. She hadn't gotten up today, but her black eyes were happy, seeing everything that went on in our house. "You are feeling better, aren't you, Gramma!" Every time I asked her, she answered, "Much better." And she never said a word about my beautiful costume, waiting in the dark under the bed.

Mama and Pop were trying to help Alberto. One was pulling his jacket down in the back, the other pulling it higher in front, while he twisted to see himself in the mirror. Suddenly Gramma's hand, the one I was holding, got funny and loose, like a doll's. Her eyes closed and her head fell on the pillow. "Mama!" I screamed. Maria Clara grabbed Sergio and Mama and Pop and all the neighbors came running to Gramma's bed. Pressing myself into the wall by the stove, I listened to everyone saying what was wrong and what to do.

"Send for the doctor!"

"You know the doctor won't come up here."

"The boys can carry her down to the ambulance," Pop said.

"Wait a little. Gramma wouldn't like the hospital. She'd want to be home," Mama told him.

132

The neighbors brought in coffee and kept telling Mama and Pop to drink. "It's *very* serious." Carolina wagged her head and clicked her tongue. "When it's time, it's time. You just get taken. Nothing anyone can do about it."

"She'll be an angel in Heaven with the Saints. No more suffering, no more troubles." Ernesto rolled his eyes up and clasped his hands together.

"Shut up!" I was in the middle of the room, shouting. "Gramma doesn't want to go to Heaven! She wants to go to Carnival!" Everyone gasped and looked at Mama.

She shook her head. "There's nothing anyone can do with *that* child."

I went near Gramma's bed, turning my back to everyone. I was talking in my head—you don't have to talk out loud because they can hear everything up there. "Listen, you're not going to get Gramma. You can't take her because I won't let you. I'll tell you what—it's just a mistake I didn't get chosen. The Director is going to come running here and say, 'It was a terrible mistake choosing Teresinha! We want *you* for Princess of the Children's Group!' And you know what I'll say to him? I'll say, 'No!' I'll give up my luck that I was born for, *if*, but only *if*, you don't take Gramma! And that's my last offer!"

Somebody sent for the Healing Man. He knows ways to cure people with tea boiled from herbs and magic and prayers. He shook a feather rattle over Gramma and muttered a long prayer. His eyes never blinked in his Indian

133

face. Then he gave Mama a blue powder to put in Gramma's tea. And, he was gone.

Pop rubbed the tears away. "She's very old, you know." I never saw Pop crying before. No, Pop! She's very young!

All that afternoon and into the evening, we sat and stood around Gramma. The bright costumes lost their colors, like the rainbow fish Nilton catches in the lagoon that turn gray at his feet.

I was saying with my heart over and over, "Oh, little Gramma, my little Gramma, don't go away and leave me. Who will stroke my hair and call me 'Good little girl'? Who will smile at me when the grown-ups are making angry faces? I won't let you go!"

But I knew from the dark hole inside me that it could happen. Unless, instead of Gramma, the Saints would take the only wonderful thing I ever had.

Boom-da, Boom-da. It was the Samba band coming up the Hill. They were parading around because they couldn't stay still and wait for tonight. The happy music marched into the room, though we tried to shut it out— "It's going to disturb Gramma!" But the music seemed to touch her eyelids. She blinked and opened her eyes. "Children, why are you standing there? You'll be late for the Avenue!"

Mama put her arms around Gramma, who was trying to get up. "Gramma, you're sick! You mustn't get up!"

Carlos, who always talks without thinking, said, "We thought you were gonna die!"

"Die?" Gramma held her head on the side like a smart little bird. "Who can die when there's another Night on the Avenue?" And she put her feet out of bed and shakily stood up.

"It's a miracle!" Pop said.

I threw my arms around her, but I didn't tell them it was *my* miracle! Gramma said, "Come, come. It's almost time. We'll be late!" And she took up Alberto's sash that she'd been working on, put a prickling row of pins between her lips, and began fitting it around him.

"It must have been a spell of faintness that went away, thank God," Pop whispered.

But Mama said, "Gramma has a very strong mind. And when she has her mind set to go to Carnival, she's going!" But I really knew—the Saints and angels had decided to accept my bargain.

After kissing Gramma on the top of her head or squeezing her, the whole family began to get ready again. It was like those funny movies where the people stop and start again, faster than before. Except me. Oh, I made myself busy, helping this one to get her feather straight, or sewing on that one's diamond that had dropped off.

But when Feijaozinbo came to get me, I would not go in the Procession. My bargain that saved Gramma was going to be kept!

"Maria Antonia!"

"Come on, you'll be late!"

The kids raced by outside, shouting for me. I peeked out of the crack of the door, but I wouldn't let them see.

"Maria Antonia, surely you're coming." Mama sounded very annoyed—the fruits and flowers on her turban wobbled as she put dry pants on Little Sergio. "Such a stubborn one, that child!"

Friends kept running in and out of the house, admiring each other and bowing to themselves in the mirror. "It's time!"

"It's time!"

137

Pop looked at me. His look said, "You'll come, I know you'll come, my good little girl." I just turned away and stared through the crack. It was *too* beautiful out there—flashing pinks and greens and gold. And people's white smiles and their skin, shined to brown satin.

"Elisabete, hurry!" Mama's friends shrieked in the window.

Carlos told me, "If you stay here, Maria Antonia, you can be Queen of the Pots and Pans." Mama smacked him, snatching up Little Sergio, and hurried to the door. Gramma followed right after her—she would hold the baby while Mama danced down the Avenue.

No one could wait any longer. The Directors were shouting for their groups to come together, to get in the proper order. "Ladies and Gentlemen! Tonight we'll show who is champion! Tonight all Rio will cheer The Cashew Tree!" Everyone began pouring down to the trains that would take them to the Avenue. Their looks at me said, "What a fool, to miss the Night on the Avenue!" Roberto, Carlos, Alberto, Maria Clara, Maria Helena, Regina, and Pop hurried out the door. They were gone, really gone. The house was quiet and gray, except for a few bright scraps of pink and green under Gramma's chair.

"*Boom-da, Boom-da!*" the band kept calling and calling. When nobody was near, I went outside on the steps. The whole hill was curving down to the City in a pink and green and gold snake of people. And the snake was dancing and singing our Samba, "The Soul of Brazil Goes

138

Forth on the Pavement Tonight." Looking around at the darkness where the other hills waited, I saw that they too were rocking to a slower Samba. Slower still the stars were dancing! The whole world was going to Carnival! Except me!

I was practicing what I would say when Feijaozinbo came running up. He would shout, "There has been a terrible mistake! *You* are the true princess of Samba! Come with me!"

"No," I'd say, sadly but proudly. "No, it is too late." (He wouldn't have to know about the bargain.) Our Samba was so far away, I could hardly hear it. The darkness came all around.

Now, honey, he's coming. I know he's coming. No, he's not!! Suddenly I knew it!! *Sure he is, honey. And if he doesn't, we'll think of something else.* . . . No, we won't! And you better stop all that "you're the best," "you were born lucky" stuff! *You said it first.* Well—*you* can stay here and argue who said it. I'm going to dance!

My bargain didn't say I couldn't be a plain dancer for The Cashew Tree. Back into the house I rushed and fell to my knees. Under the bed—there it was, the plastic bag with my costume. Quickly, quickly, into the beautiful, slippery pink-and-green dress. My shoes?! Oh, where?! There—waiting on Gramma's rocker where I had to see them.

Holding the pink slippers in my hand so they wouldn't get muddy, I jumped out the door without touching the steps. Down the path, faster, faster, till the houses and gardens and wash lines seemed to be running past me.

"Wait! Wait!" I prayed. "Oh, please don't go without me!" Now I saw the officials in their black suits and white fronts, serious as beetles; they belong at the end of the Procession, so I was not too late! Where was the Children's Group in all this pink-and-green ocean?! I couldn't push past the officials; they're too important. I stood on the tips of my toes; no use. So, I just jumped into "the ocean." Here and there I was carried, squashed in the crowd. But at least I was being squashed toward the trains.

Joking people were pushing one another onto the train, and I felt myself lifted under the arms. "Up and in, little girl!" Next to a shaking pink-and-green mountain was where I ended up. The mountain groaned and laughed by turns—it was Lindomar! She kept her little husband under her arm like a mama chicken and its chick. And when she saw that he could hardly breathe pressed in so tight, she took in a great big breath and pushed everybody back.

We waited, close together as beans in a sack.

With a crash, the train jerked forward, then back. It was going! Swaying and rattling, it carried us toward the City, toward the Avenue!

Another crash! The swaying stopped, the doors opened. Those near them fell out and others climbed through the windows to the station. Lindomar put me and her

140

husband out a window, but she had to wait to take her skirts sideways through the door when the car was empty.

For a moment, I couldn't tell where we were. The City seemed all dark, except that far away there was a long, glowing line. Maybe the City was burning?! No! How dumb I was! It was the Avenue President Vargas, and all the people were hurrying there.

The beautiful pink-and-green Cashew Tree was all around, carrying me forward. Other Samba groups ran into ours—Salgueiro's foamy red-and-white ruffles, Portela's blue-and-white stripes. Down a dark side street, green-and-white capes rippled like fish swimming by.

I felt so good! For the first time in *so long*, I wasn't worrying about Teresinha. Just to dance, that's all I wanted. And I was going to do it!

It was not possible to get lost—one just had to follow the big ferryboat, Lindomar. She was bobbing ahead on pink-and-green waves. But my kids, how could I ever find the kids' group among two thousand people in time to dance with them down the Avenue?!

"Aaawahhh!" A gang of naked-chested Indians waved their hatchets and jumped up and down, making a ring around me. They made terrible noises, but their faces were too happy to scare anybody. "Hey! Let me go! I have to follow my people!" The Cashew Tree was disappearing in the dark between the high buildings! The Indians moved off to capture someone else. I ran where I'd last seen it—but there wasn't a bit of pink and green!

141

A palace stood in front of me, all made of pretty carved stone. Straight glass buildings poked up high all around it, but this palace was grander than any. From its balconies and windows, music and yellow light spilled down on the people below.

A long, shiny black-licorice car swung around to the wide stone steps. Sitting in it was The Snow Queen! Her diamond dress filled all the seats of the black car, and when the driver opened the door, she poured out like snow sliding down. (I know about snow from the T.V. It's like vanilla ice cream.) How beautiful she was! I came close enough to hear her say, "Ai! My skirt is getting crushed!" She hurried, frowning, into the palace with the dress icing the steps behind her.

"You crazy!" I hit my forehead. "You have to find the kids before they go on the Avenue without you!" Which way? I tagged after the "Better Than Whiskey" Samba band. Maybe they'd take me to the Avenue. But they had laughed and played so much that they fell in the street, sleeping, one fellow's head in the next one's lap.

Now I could hear the noise like a giant's mouth roaring—it was the people on the Avenue cheering. Maybe they were cheering The Cashew Tree?! Oh, why didn't I go with my kids? Why was I so stubborn? I'm a real baby, like Nilton said. The tears began sneaking down.

"Little girl, are you lost?" A small man, like Pop, stood there with country clothes and a farmer's straw hat. His whole family stood around him—Mama, Grampa, and many little children. They stood aside from all the jumping and singing, but they looked with wonder at the crowds. "We came from outside Rio to see Carnival. You are welcome to stay with us till you find your folks."

"Thank you, I'm not lost. I'm one of the dancers of The Cashew Tree and I'm going to the Avenue. Thank you all the same, and I hope you enjoy Carnival."

As if I knew just where to go, I moved into the crowd.

When they couldn't see me anymore, I dashed the tears away.

"Please, can you tell me how to get to the Avenue?"

"Urrow!" The dancing cat spun around, and when she saw it was me who had pulled her tail, she pointed a paw. "That way." Grinning clowns, tramps, hula girls, and laughing skeletons bumped and pushed me this way, then that way. "Oh, stop! Stop!" How could they be so happy when I was so miserable? I'd never find my friends, never help The Cashew Tree to win! And to make it worse, the Beatles (that is, four boys with rubber Beatle faces) took hold of my hands and would not let go.

"Psst, Maria Antonia!" Ducking under Paul's arm, tripping Ringo so that he let go of me, Nilton stood there grinning!

"Oh, Nilton! How did you find me?"

"Never mind. Come on, it's not far. There's still time." He pulled me down one alley after another, where the silent cats stared at us; only Nilton knows all these back parts of Rio.

Embarrassed, I looked sideways at him. I almost said, "And how is your girl friend, Teresinha?" Instead I asked, "How did you know I would come?"

"You're dumb, but you're not really so dumb as you act—come on!"

Darker than the night, a great shape came before us. The grandstand on the Avenue! Golden light and cheers showered up from it into the black sky. But right in front of it, a fence of policemen in brown uniforms! They stood with feet apart, looking straight ahead. And they stayed silent as wood when we asked, "Please, who is dancing now, Mr. Policeman?"

Then a voice came down from inside the white helmet. "It's The Cashew Tree, isn't it, Hector?"

Another white helmet spoke, "That's right. I'll bet they're the champions."

"Oh," I screamed, "that's us! You've got to let us in!"

"If you don't pay, you can't get in. So beat it!"

It was no use. We moved back. Nilton's eyes ran here and there and stopped at a little pair of white shorts disappearing beneath the grandstand, right behind the policeman. Pretending we were going away, we turned and ducked under, after the white pants.

For a minute it was too dark to see. But the black was striped with light—from the Avenue! Then we saw kids creeping around among the soda bottles and garbage. Quickly we crawled toward the light, bumping our heads on the board seats above.

It was like a colored movie going by between all the legs and feet. The Cashew Tree was out there, showing what our people could do! "Oh, Nilton, we're so beautiful!" I sighed. Then I screamed, "Oh, look, look! I see her! I see her! It's Wilma!" She was there in the front, smiling like a Queen, dipping the banner, never forgetting how a Queen has to be. Her Escort leaped and bowed

145

around her, as clever and quick as his sword. And everybody else was dancing like crazy pink-and-green angels.

The black-and-white officials came now, so very dignified, lifting their tall black hats to the cheering crowd, smiling to one side and the other. Nilton poked me. "Mr. Alberto Nascimento is escorting his stomach." It was true! He did look like that. *Boom-da! Boom-da!* the band played louder and faster, and the faster they played, the faster The Cashew Tree danced.

The people in the grandstands cheered for the young men. Their legs bent like spaghettis, moving faster than your eyes could believe. They cheered for the ladies whose trains were so heavy with jewels they could only take little, half-dancing steps. The shepherdesses—I saw Maria Clara, Maria Helena, and Regina—made everybody whistle and sigh. All the men wanted to be their boyfriends.

Nilton reached into a picnic basket next to a rich man's leg. He took out a bit of cheese, a big slice of ham, and a curl of lettuce for a sandwich. But I couldn't eat. I had to get out there! Wriggling between a lady's fat ankles, stuffed in pointy-heel shoes, I fell out—onto the Avenue!

Louisa screamed, "Maria Antonia!"

"Don't stop!" the Director shouted. With his big, round eyes and green suit all shiny with sweat, he looked like an important frog, jumping everywhere and blowing his whistle. He cried, "Go, my beauties, go! Dance till your feet wear away the asphalt!"

146

I took my place and we danced as if we were going up to heaven. Teresinha was there in the front somewhere, but I didn't even look.

All over the mile of the Avenue we danced, till our hearts beat louder than the music. A sudden rain dumped down; it only cooled us so we could dance hotter than before.

When 2,000 of us had gone past the judges and out into the darkness again, we flopped down on the curbs and in the streets. Laughing and crying and gasping, we held on to each other.

"Oh, my sweet life!" Caroline wept.

Louisa was hugging me and everybody around her. "We were so good!" she kept saying.

Damon was looking surprised not to be worried. A cool, sweet peace came on us. We were remembering it all over again like a wonderful dream. Nilton sat next to me on the curb. I smiled and smiled, too happy to speak.

"Listen to this, Maria Antonia. You know that part when the Emperor salutes the people?"

I nodded.

"You know how the band plays to a big crash and then stops so it's quiet for a minute?"

I nodded again.

"Well, I was near the Judges' Stand, and I could hear them talking—I went really near to see that T.V. star with the wavy hair, you know, Reynaldo—and I heard a judge, maybe the Director of Tourism, say . . ."

147

I was not really listening; there was still dancing inside of me.

Nilton went on: "The Director of Tourism—I think it was him—said, 'Look at that little one. How she can dance!' 'That one?' Reynaldo asked, and he pointed at Teresinha. 'No, not her. The one in back with the cute little ponytail!' "

Now I was listening.

"He pointed at you, Maria Antonia! Then he said, 'She has that look. They have to have it to be Queen. You know, my dear Reynaldo, I think we *may* be looking at the next one to carry the flag for The Cashew Tree . . . the next Queen of the Samba!' "

Nilton looked so proud of me. And I was glad the people said that. But the important thing—oh, I don't know how to say it—Gramma and Mama and me and my little baby, we're going to dance Samba forever!

About the Author

MIRIAM COHEN fell in love with Carnival and Samba in the two years that she and her family lived in Brazil. Attending a conference on the problems of slum children, she heard someone say, "You tell us all the things these children haven't got, but you don't mention the beautiful things they do have: their expressiveness, their marvelous talent for dance and drama." BORN TO DANCE SAMBA is her tribute to the vitality of spirit in those children.

The author of more than ten picture books, Ms. Cohen now lives with her husband in Brooklyn, New York.

About the Artist

GIOIA FIAMMENGHI is the illustrator of over fifty books for children, and her work has been exhibited in both the United States and France. Having traveled widely, including some long visits in Colombia, South America, she and her entire family speak English, French, Italian, and Spanish. Ms. Fiammenghi currently lives in Nice, France.